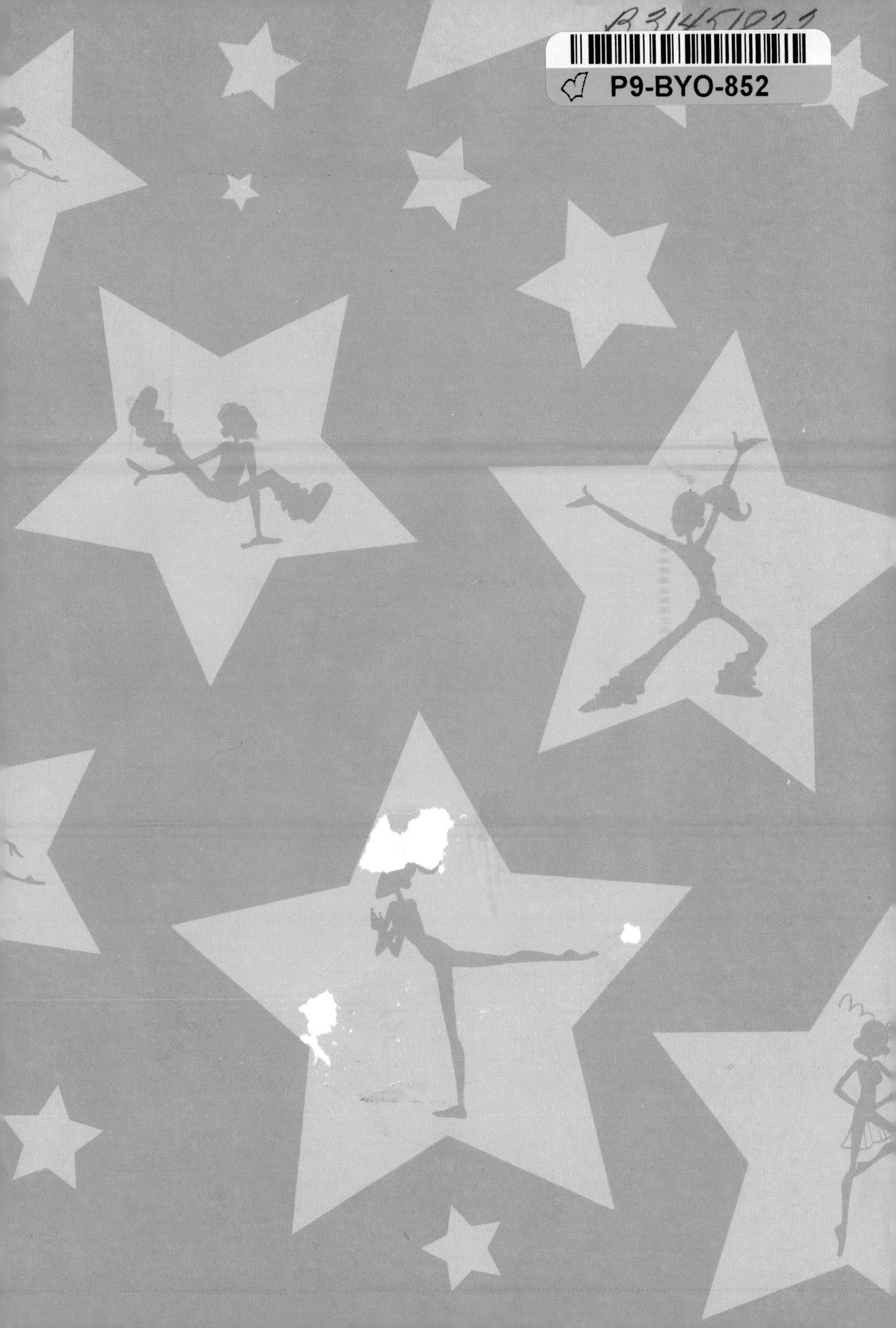

# Dance Class

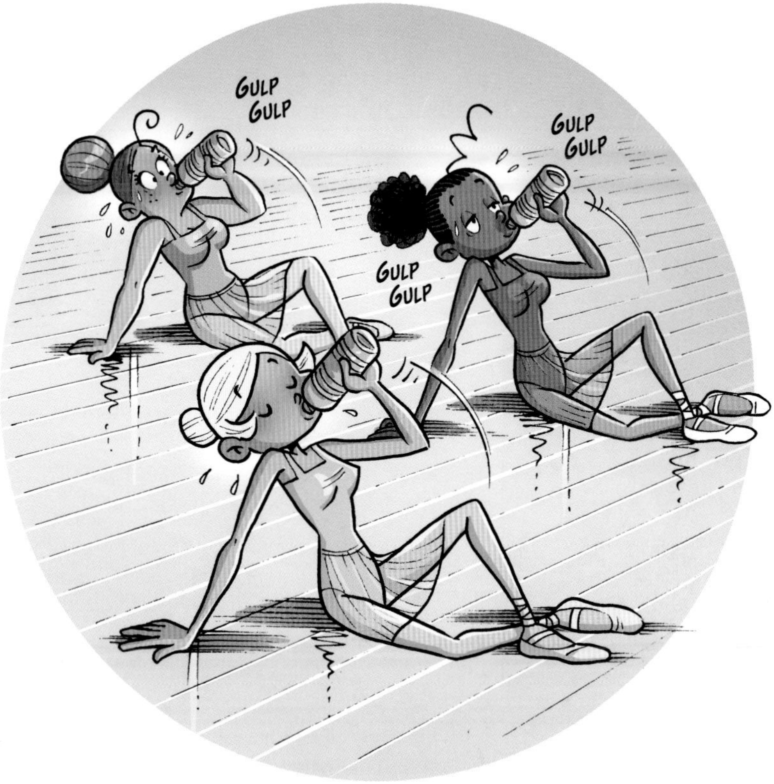
GULP
GULP
GULP
GULP
GULP
GULP

Crip • Art

Béka • Story

Maëla Cosson • Color



PAPERCUTZ™
New York

# Dance Class Graphic Novels Available from PAPERCUTZ™

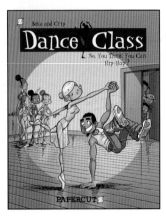

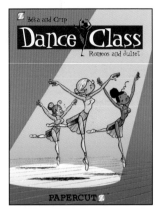

Béka and Crip
Dance Class
So, You Think You Can Hip-Hop?
PAPERCUTZ

#1 "So, You Think You Can Hip-Hop?"

Béka and Crip
Dance Class
Romeos and Juliet
PAPERCUTZ

#2 "Romeos and Juliet"

Coming Soon!

Béka and Crip
Dance Class
African Folk Fever
PAPERCUTZ

#3 "African Folk Fever"



# Dance Class



DANCE CLASS #2
"Romeos and Juliet"

Béka - writer
Crip - Artist
Maëla Cosson - Colorist
Joe Johnson - Translation
Tom Orzechowski - Lettering
Masheka Wood - Production
Sylvia Nantier - Dance Consultant
Michael Petranek - Associate Editor
Jim Salicrup
Editor-in-Chief

ISBN: 978-1-59707-317-2

Printed in China
May 2012 by New Era Printing Ltd.
Trend Centre, 29-31 Cheung Lee St.
Rm.1101-1103, 11/F
Chaiwan, Hong Kong

Distributed by Macmillan
First Papercutz Printing

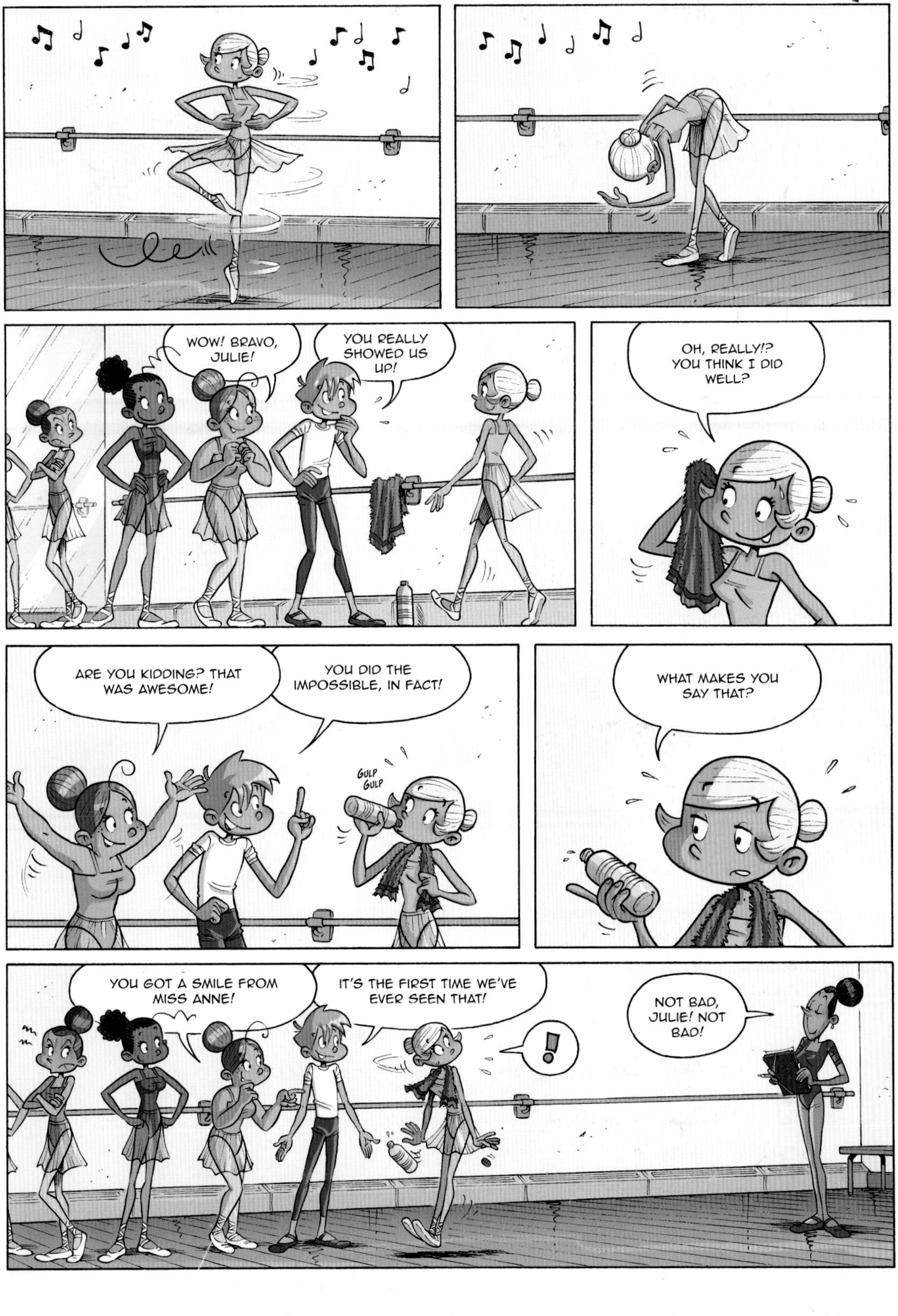
WOW! BRAVO, JULIE!
YOU REALLY SHOWED US UP!
OH, REALLY!? YOU THINK I DID WELL?
ARE YOU KIDDING? THAT WAS AWESOME!
YOU DID THE IMPOSSIBLE, IN FACT!
GULP GULP
WHAT MAKES YOU SAY THAT?
YOU GOT A SMILE FROM MISS ANNE!
IT'S THE FIRST TIME WE'VE EVER SEEN THAT!
!
NOT BAD, JULIE! NOT BAD!

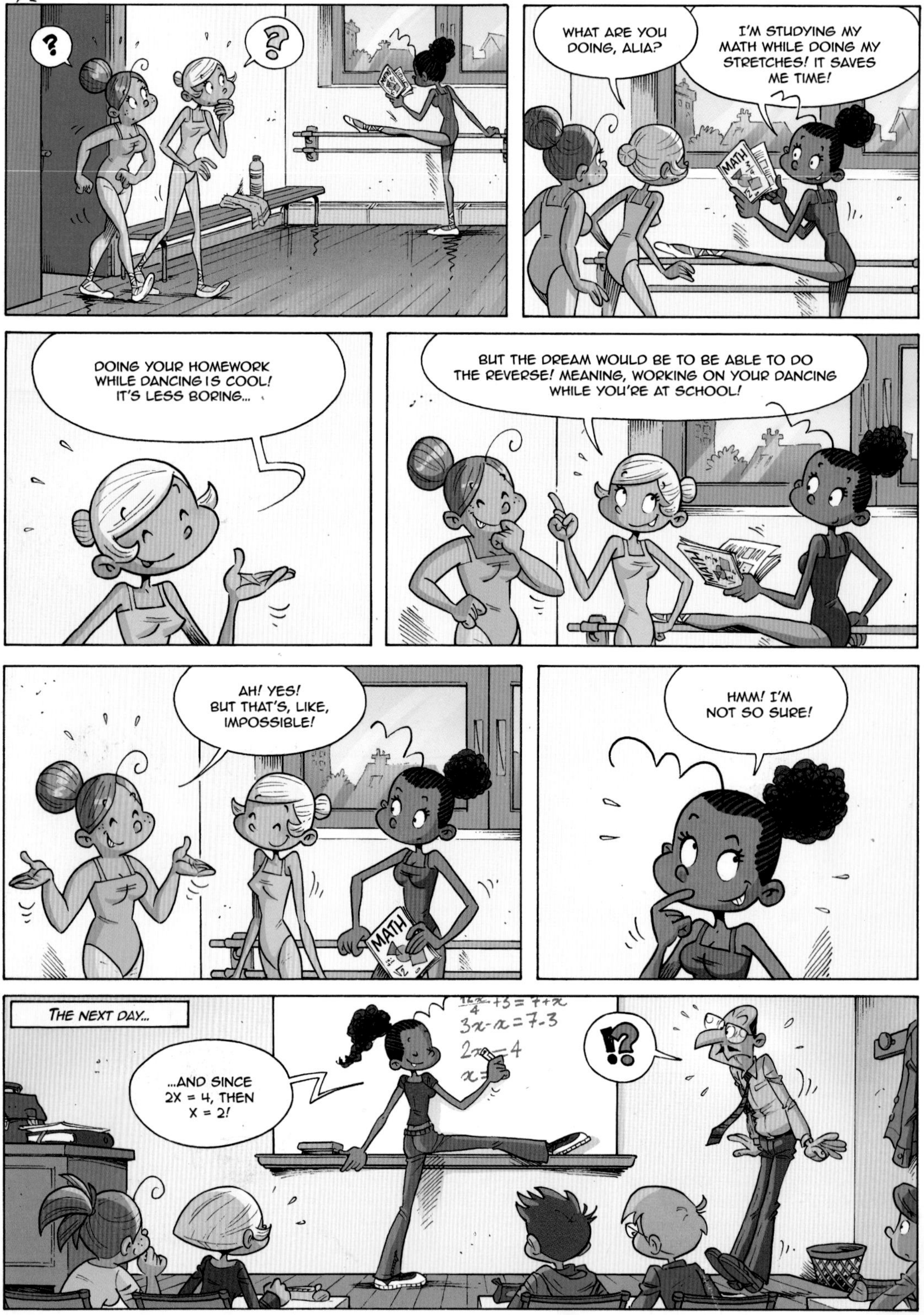
?
?
WHAT ARE YOU DOING, ALIA?
I'M STUDYING MY MATH WHILE DOING MY STRETCHES! IT SAVES ME TIME!
DOING YOUR HOMEWORK WHILE DANCING IS COOL! IT'S LESS BORING...
BUT THE DREAM WOULD BE TO BE ABLE TO DO THE REVERSE! MEANING, WORKING ON YOUR DANCING WHILE YOU'RE AT SCHOOL!
AH! YES! BUT THAT'S, LIKE, IMPOSSIBLE!
HMM! I'M NOT SO SURE!
THE NEXT DAY...
3x-x=7-3
2x=4
...AND SINCE 2X = 4, THEN X = 2!
!?

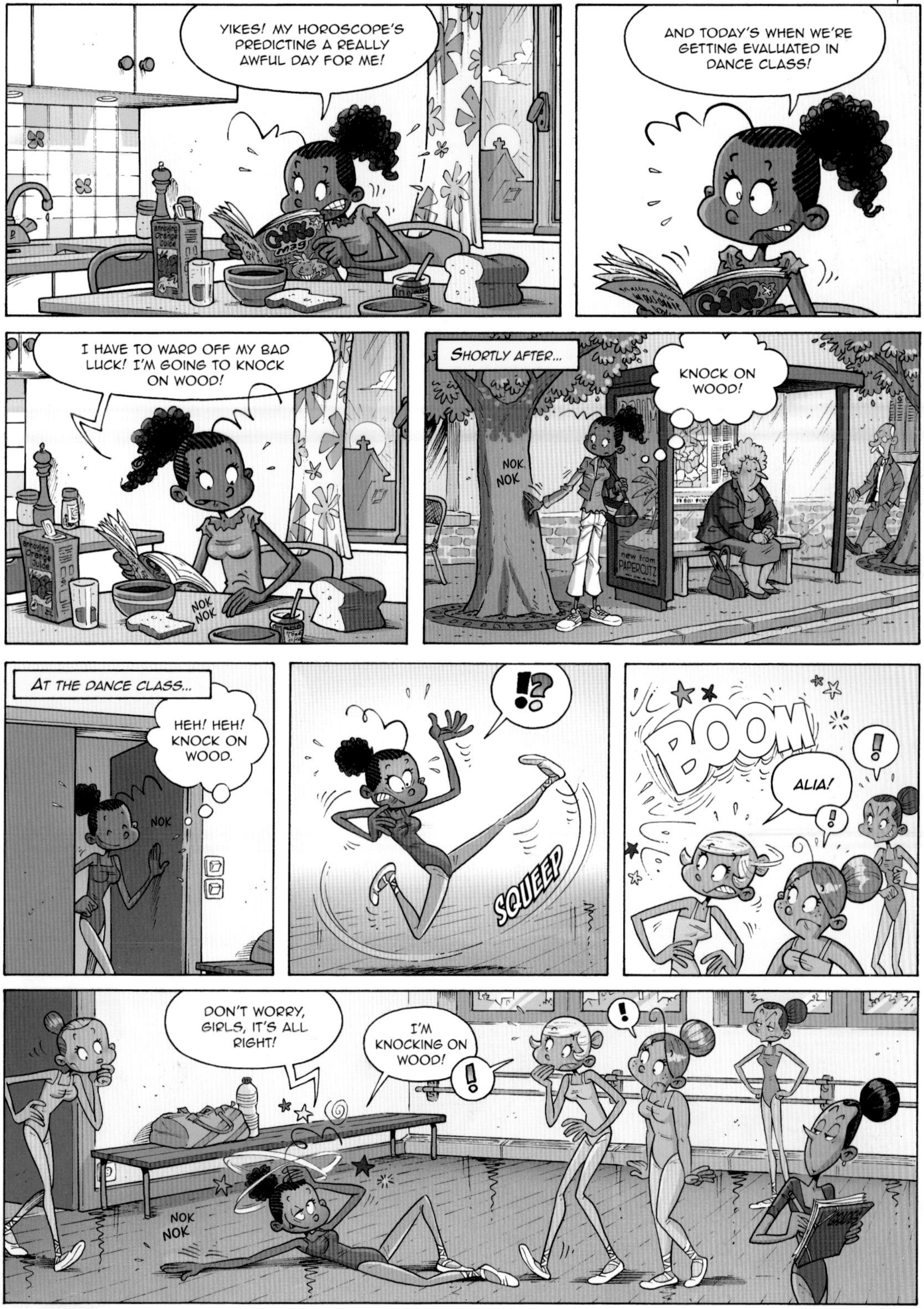
YIKES! MY HOROSCOPE'S PREDICTING A REALLY AWFUL DAY FOR ME!
AND TODAY'S WHEN WE'RE GETTING EVALUATED IN DANCE CLASS!
I HAVE TO WARD OFF MY BAD LUCK! I'M GOING TO KNOCK ON WOOD!
NOK NOK
SHORTLY AFTER...
KNOCK ON WOOD!
NOK NOK
new from PAPERCUTZ
AT THE DANCE CLASS...
HEH! HEH! KNOCK ON WOOD.
NOK
!?
SQUEEP
BOOM
!
ALIA!
!
DON'T WORRY, GIRLS, IT'S ALL RIGHT!
I'M KNOCKING ON WOOD!
!
!
NOK NOK

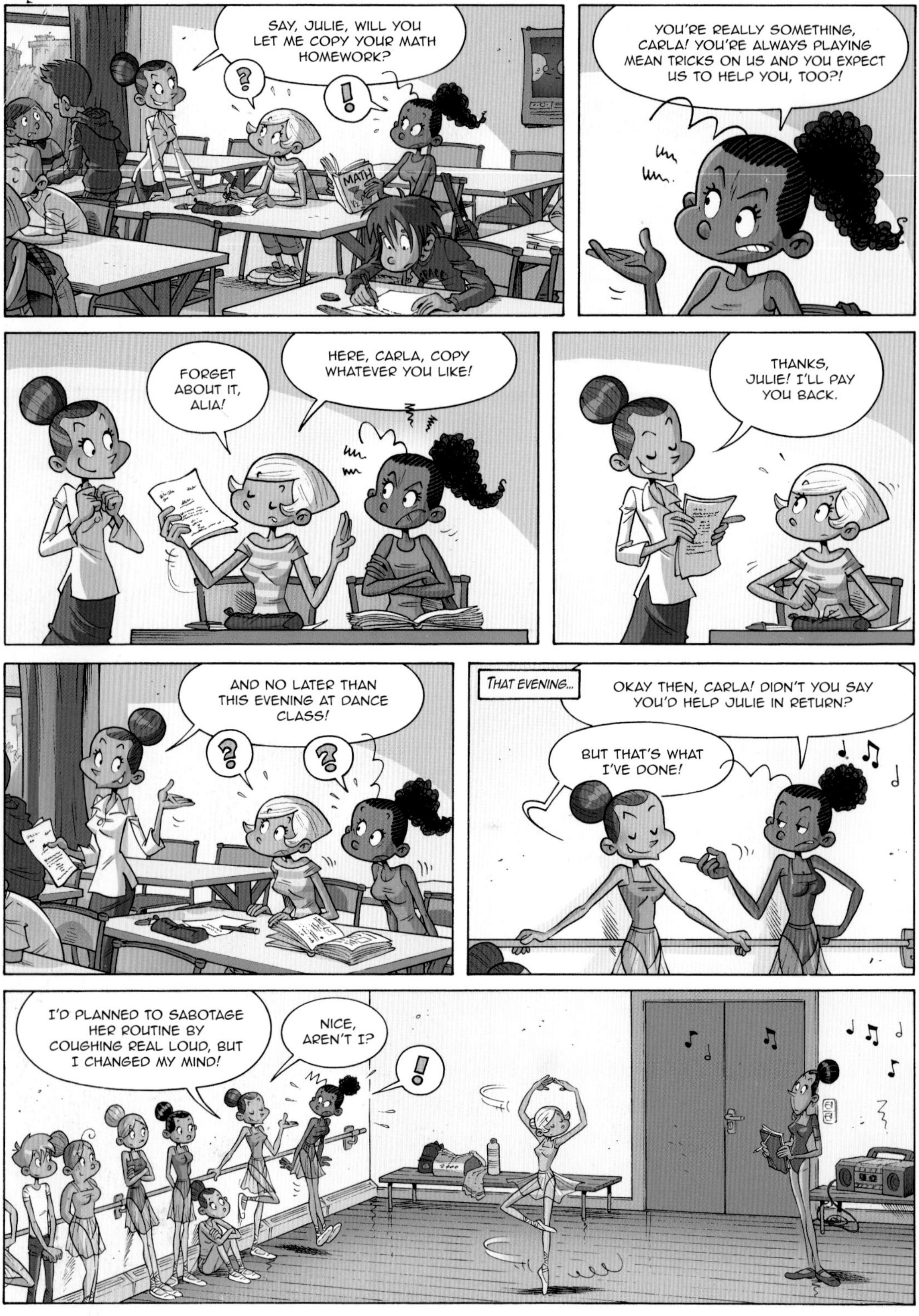
SAY, JULIE, WILL YOU LET ME COPY YOUR MATH HOMEWORK?
?
!
MATH
YOU'RE REALLY SOMETHING, CARLA! YOU'RE ALWAYS PLAYING MEAN TRICKS ON US AND YOU EXPECT US TO HELP YOU, TOO?!
FORGET ABOUT IT, ALIA!
HERE, CARLA, COPY WHATEVER YOU LIKE!
THANKS, JULIE! I'LL PAY YOU BACK.
AND NO LATER THAN THIS EVENING AT DANCE CLASS!
?
?
THAT EVENING...
OKAY THEN, CARLA! DIDN'T YOU SAY YOU'D HELP JULIE IN RETURN?
BUT THAT'S WHAT I'VE DONE!
I'D PLANNED TO SABOTAGE HER ROUTINE BY COUGHING REAL LOUD, BUT I CHANGED MY MIND!
NICE, AREN'T I?
!

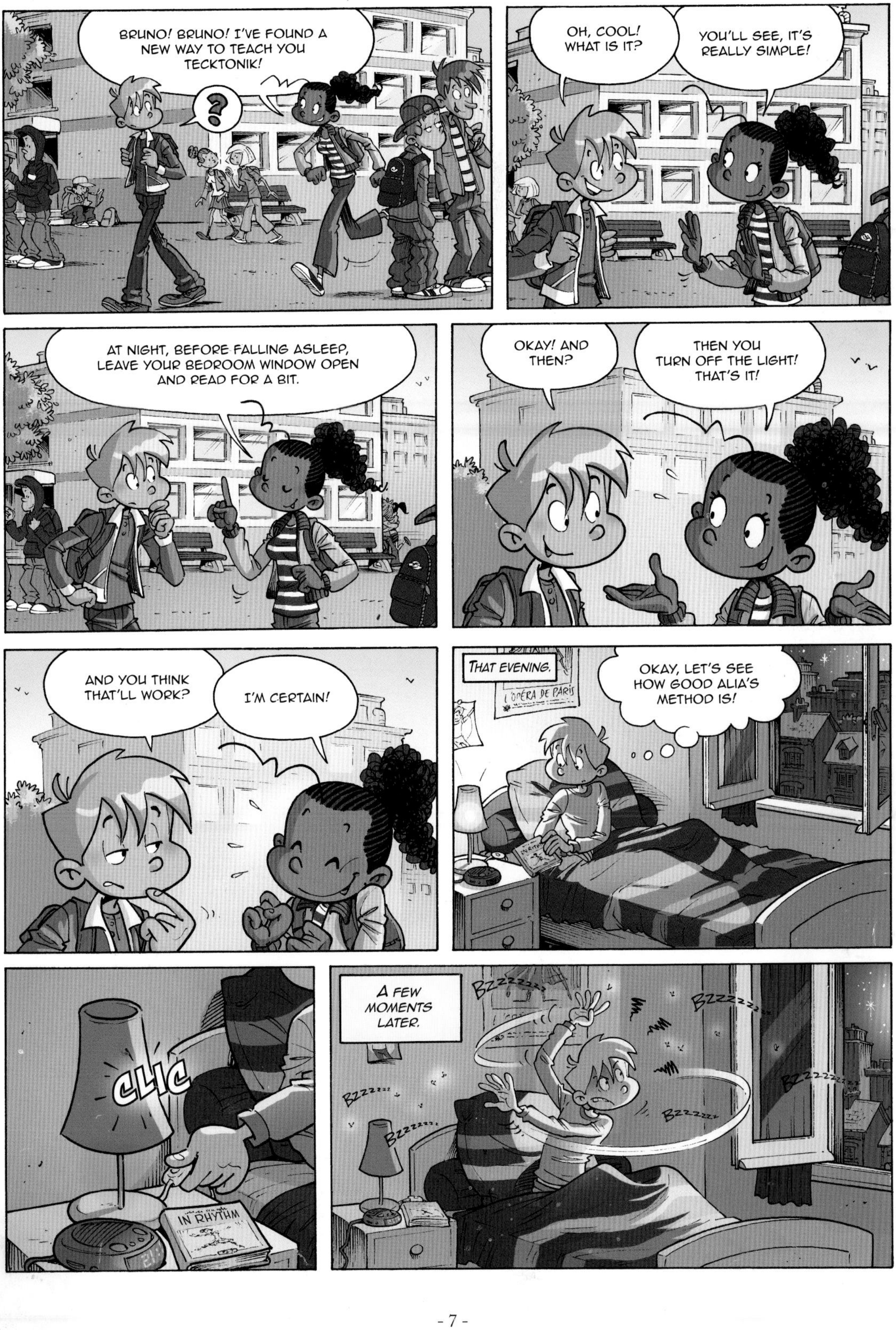
BRUNO! BRUNO! I'VE FOUND A NEW WAY TO TEACH YOU TECKTONIK!
?
OH, COOL! WHAT IS IT?
YOU'LL SEE, IT'S REALLY SIMPLE!
AT NIGHT, BEFORE FALLING ASLEEP, LEAVE YOUR BEDROOM WINDOW OPEN AND READ FOR A BIT.
OKAY! AND THEN?
THEN YOU TURN OFF THE LIGHT! THAT'S IT!
AND YOU THINK THAT'LL WORK?
I'M CERTAIN!
THAT EVENING.
L'OPÉRA DE PARIS
OKAY, LET'S SEE HOW GOOD ALIA'S METHOD IS!
CLIC
IN RHYTHM
A FEW MOMENTS LATER.
BZZZZZZZ
BZZZZZZZZ
BZZZZZZZ
BZZZZZZZ
BZZZZZZZZZ
BZZZZZZ

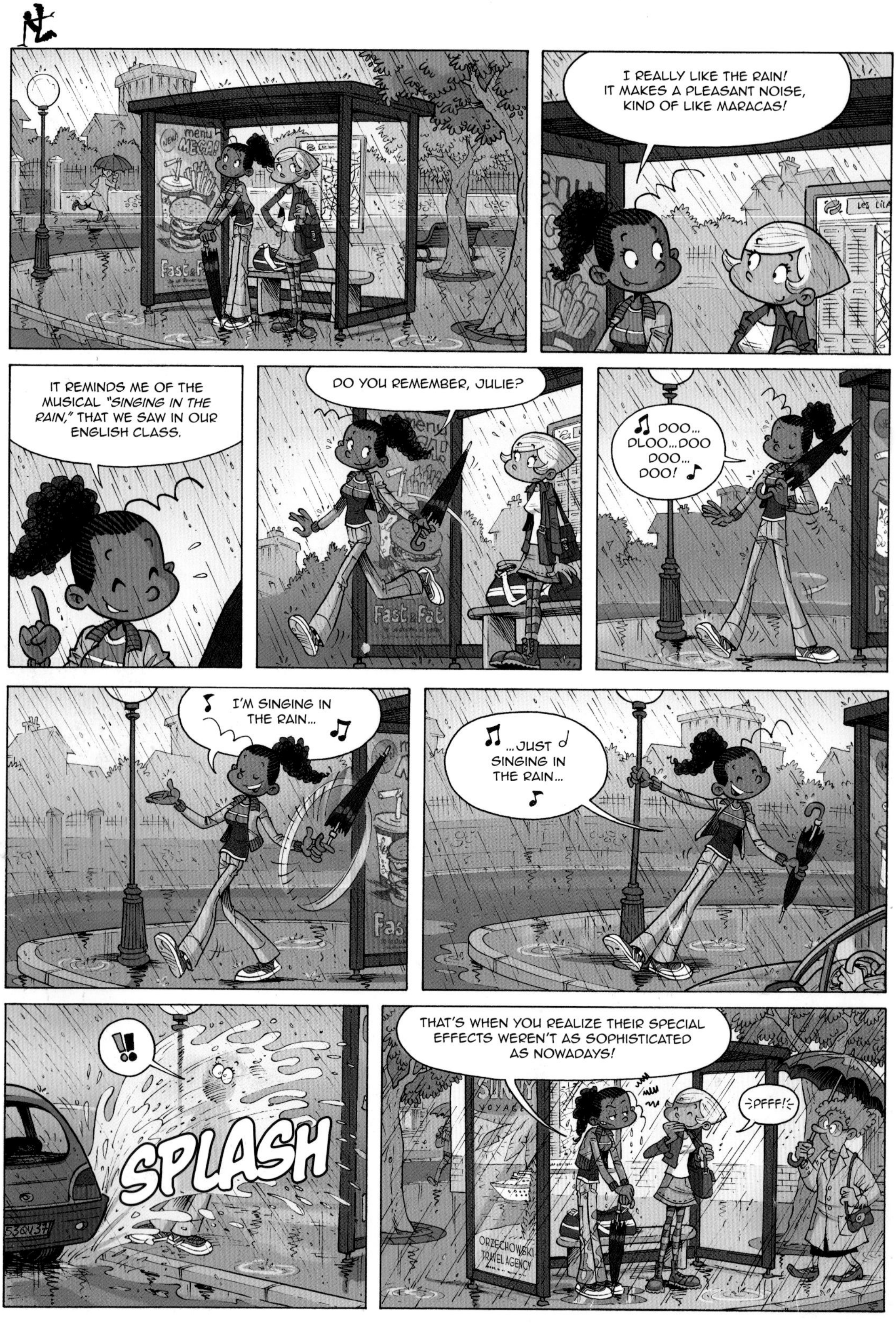
menu MEGA!
Fast & Fat
I REALLY LIKE THE RAIN! IT MAKES A PLEASANT NOISE, KIND OF LIKE MARACAS!
IT REMINDS ME OF THE MUSICAL *"SINGING IN THE RAIN,"* THAT WE SAW IN OUR ENGLISH CLASS.
DO YOU REMEMBER, JULIE?
DOO... DLOO...DOO DOO... DOO!
I'M SINGING IN THE RAIN...
...JUST SINGING IN THE RAIN...
!!
SPLASH
THAT'S WHEN YOU REALIZE THEIR SPECIAL EFFECTS WEREN'T AS SOPHISTICATED AS NOWADAYS!
PFFF!
ORZECHOWSKI TRAVEL AGENCY

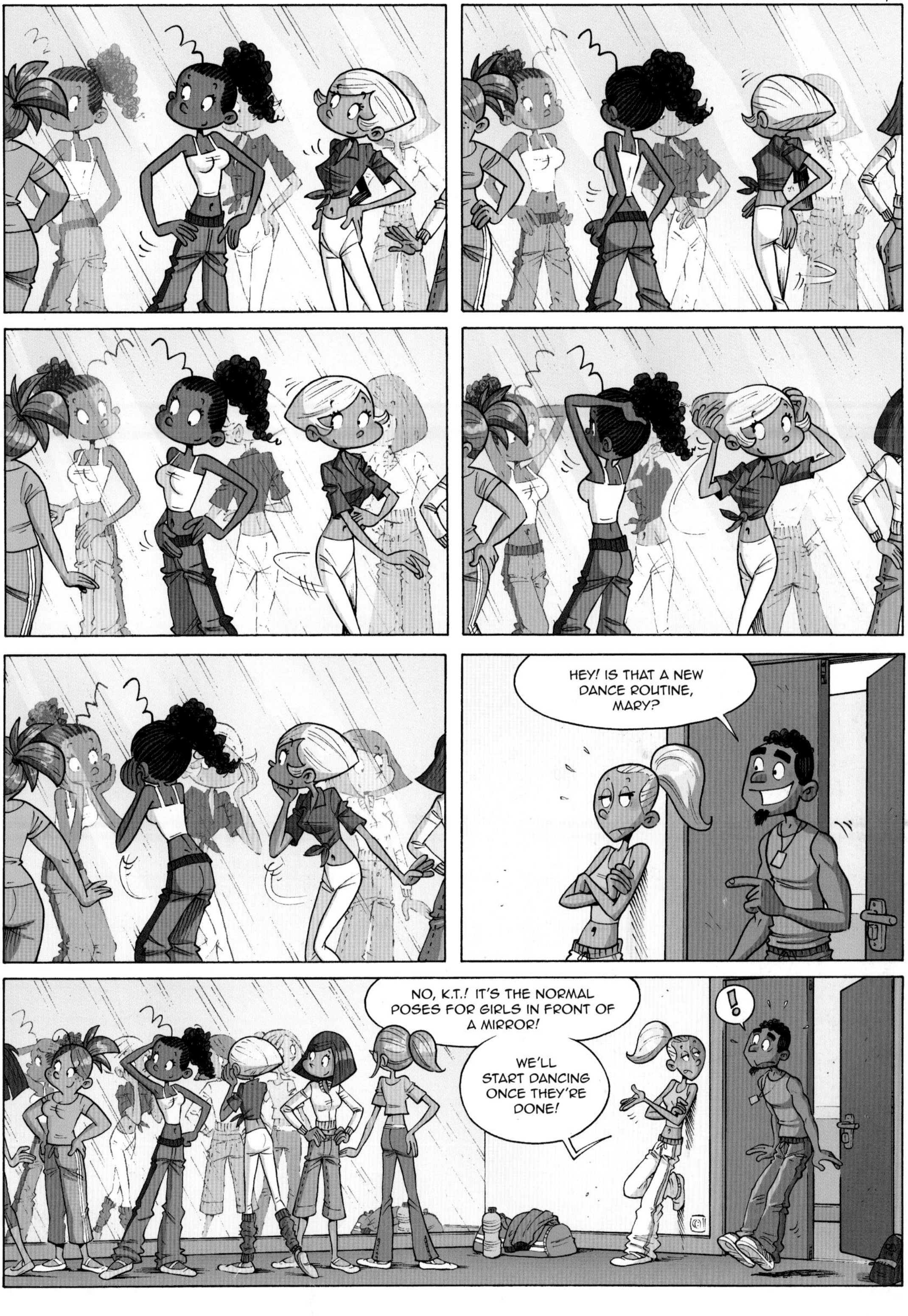
HEY! IS THAT A NEW DANCE ROUTINE, MARY?
!
NO, K.T.! IT'S THE NORMAL POSES FOR GIRLS IN FRONT OF A MIRROR!
WE'LL START DANCING ONCE THEY'RE DONE!

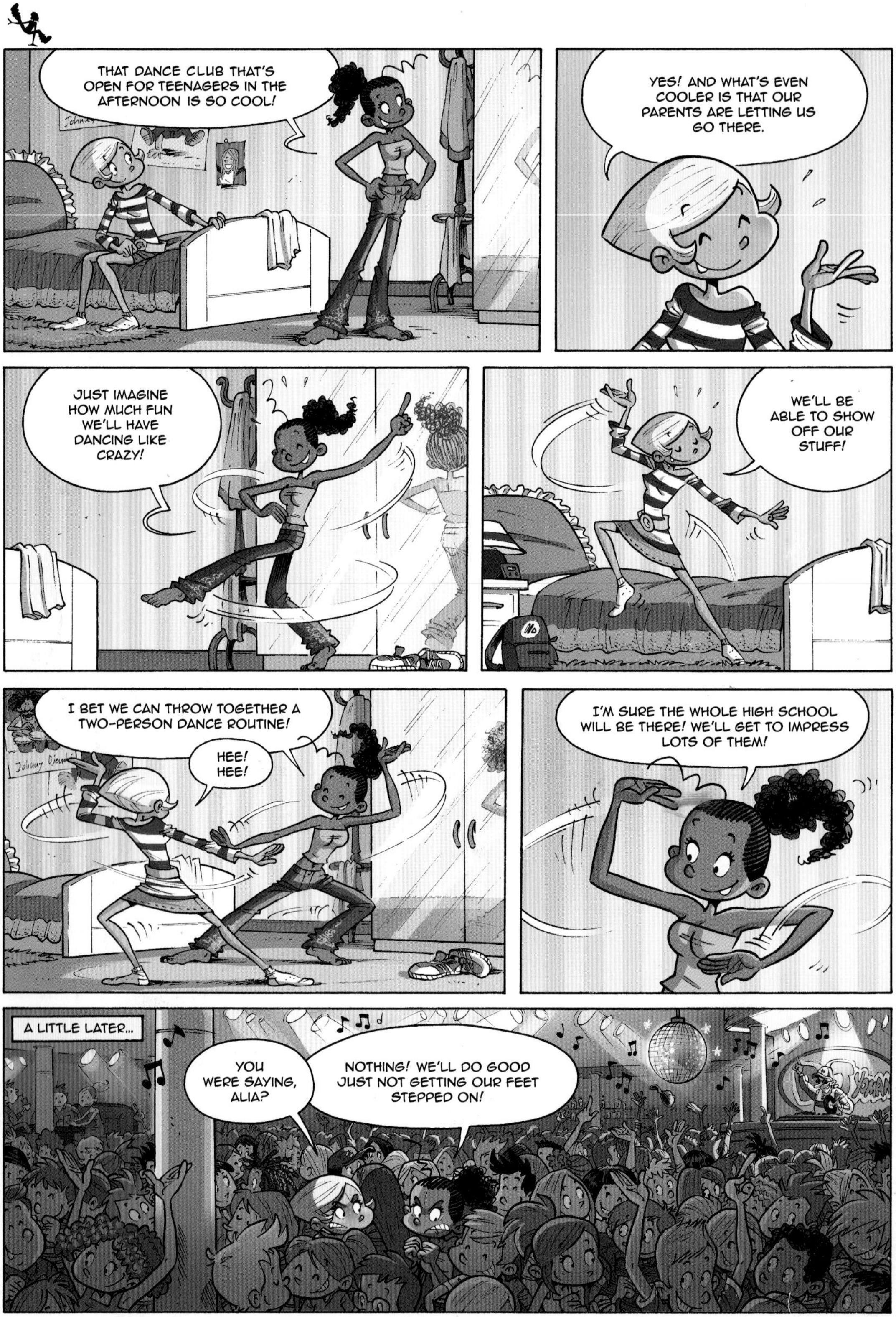

THAT DANCE CLUB THAT'S OPEN FOR TEENAGERS IN THE AFTERNOON IS SO COOL!
YES! AND WHAT'S EVEN COOLER IS THAT OUR PARENTS ARE LETTING US GO THERE.
JUST IMAGINE HOW MUCH FUN WE'LL HAVE DANCING LIKE CRAZY!
WE'LL BE ABLE TO SHOW OFF OUR STUFF!
I BET WE CAN THROW TOGETHER A TWO-PERSON DANCE ROUTINE!
HEE! HEE!
I'M SURE THE WHOLE HIGH SCHOOL WILL BE THERE! WE'LL GET TO IMPRESS LOTS OF THEM!
A LITTLE LATER...
YOU WERE SAYING, ALIA?
NOTHING! WE'LL DO GOOD JUST NOT GETTING OUR FEET STEPPED ON!

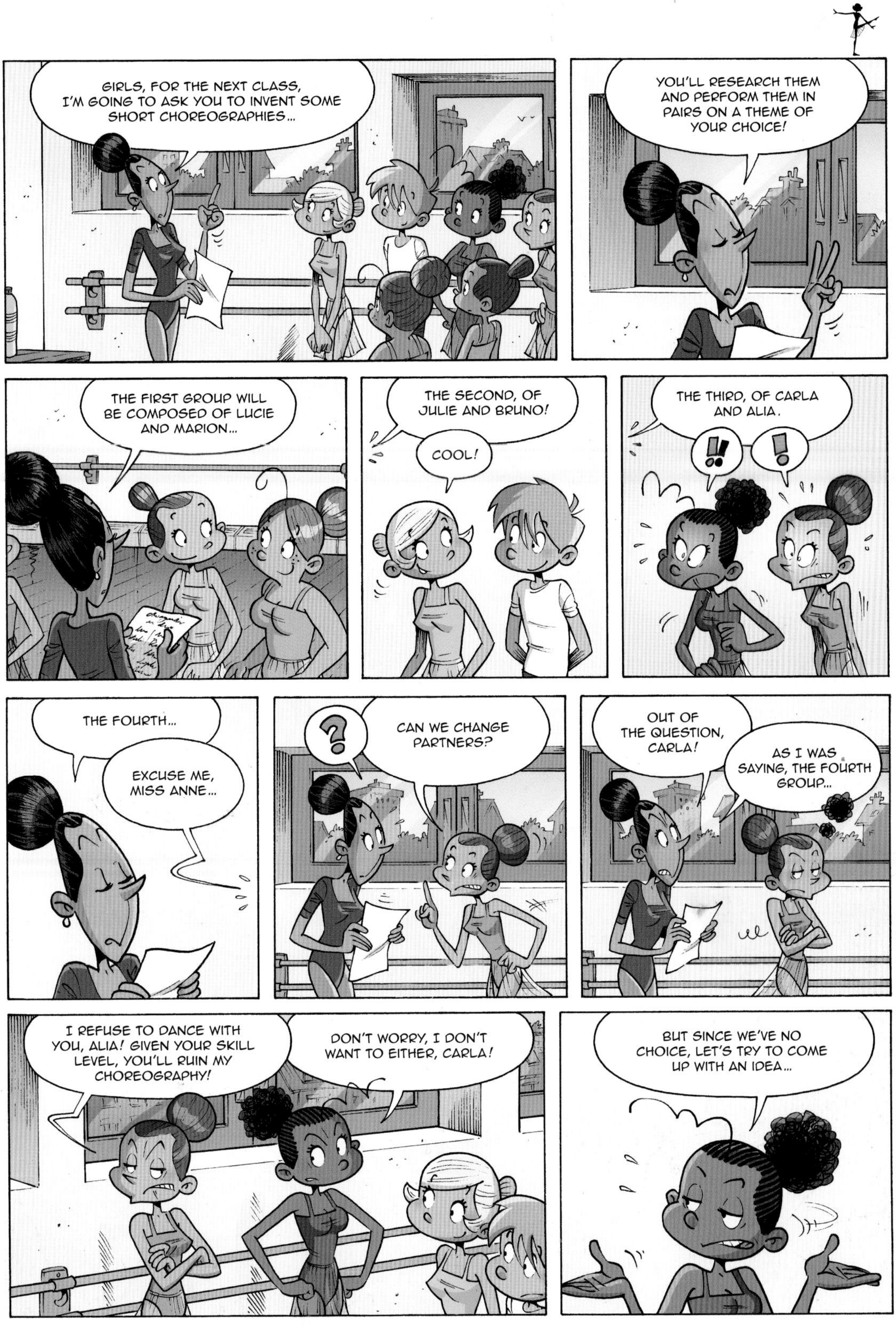
GIRLS, FOR THE NEXT CLASS, I'M GOING TO ASK YOU TO INVENT SOME SHORT CHOREOGRAPHIES...
YOU'LL RESEARCH THEM AND PERFORM THEM IN PAIRS ON A THEME OF YOUR CHOICE!
THE FIRST GROUP WILL BE COMPOSED OF LUCIE AND MARION...
THE SECOND, OF JULIE AND BRUNO!
COOL!
THE THIRD, OF CARLA AND ALIA.
!!
!
THE FOURTH...
EXCUSE ME, MISS ANNE...
?
CAN WE CHANGE PARTNERS?
OUT OF THE QUESTION, CARLA!
AS I WAS SAYING, THE FOURTH GROUP...
I REFUSE TO DANCE WITH YOU, ALIA! GIVEN YOUR SKILL LEVEL, YOU'LL RUIN MY CHOREOGRAPHY!
DON'T WORRY, I DON'T WANT TO EITHER, CARLA!
BUT SINCE WE'VE NO CHOICE, LET'S TRY TO COME UP WITH AN IDEA...

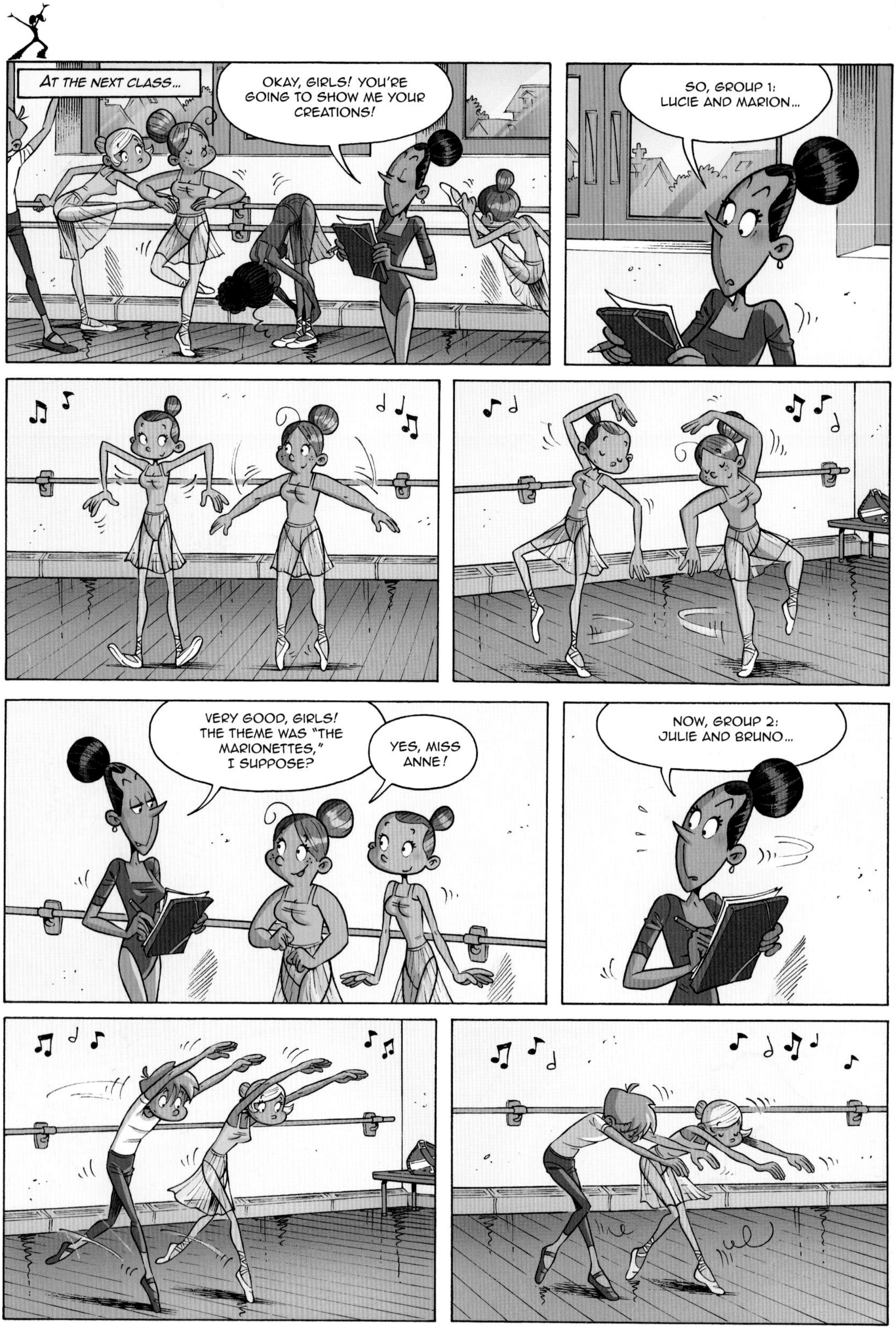

AT THE NEXT CLASS...
OKAY, GIRLS! YOU'RE GOING TO SHOW ME YOUR CREATIONS!
SO, GROUP 1: LUCIE AND MARION...
VERY GOOD, GIRLS! THE THEME WAS "THE MARIONETTES," I SUPPOSE?
YES, MISS ANNE!
NOW, GROUP 2: JULIE AND BRUNO...

MAGNIFICENT! I THOUGHT I SAW CRASHING WAVES!

OUR THEME WAS A "TEMPEST AT SEA," MISS ANNE!

YOUR TURN, CARLA AND ALIA!

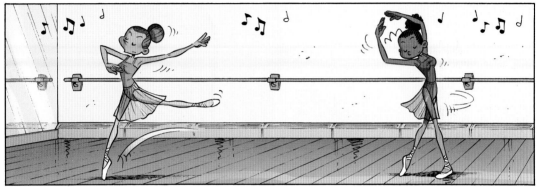

WELL, I DON'T GET IT! WHAT THEME DID YOU CHOOSE?

DISAGREEMENT!

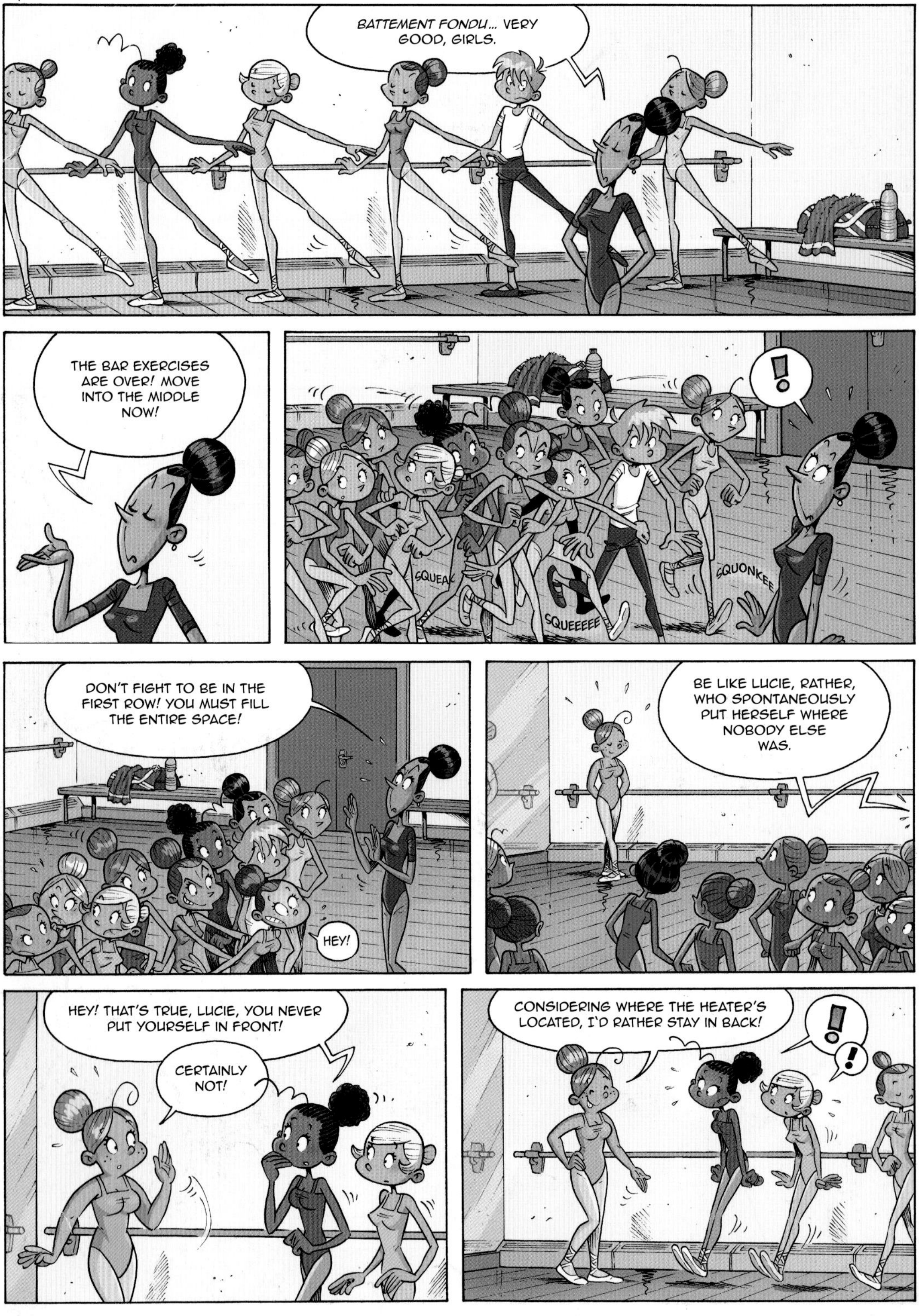
BATTEMENT FONDU... VERY GOOD, GIRLS.
THE BAR EXERCISES ARE OVER! MOVE INTO THE MIDDLE NOW!
!
SQUEAK
SQUEEEEE
SQUONKEE
DON'T FIGHT TO BE IN THE FIRST ROW! YOU MUST FILL THE ENTIRE SPACE!
HEY!
BE LIKE LUCIE, RATHER, WHO SPONTANEOUSLY PUT HERSELF WHERE NOBODY ELSE WAS.
HEY! THAT'S TRUE, LUCIE, YOU NEVER PUT YOURSELF IN FRONT!
CERTAINLY NOT!
CONSIDERING WHERE THE HEATER'S LOCATED, I'D RATHER STAY IN BACK!
!
!

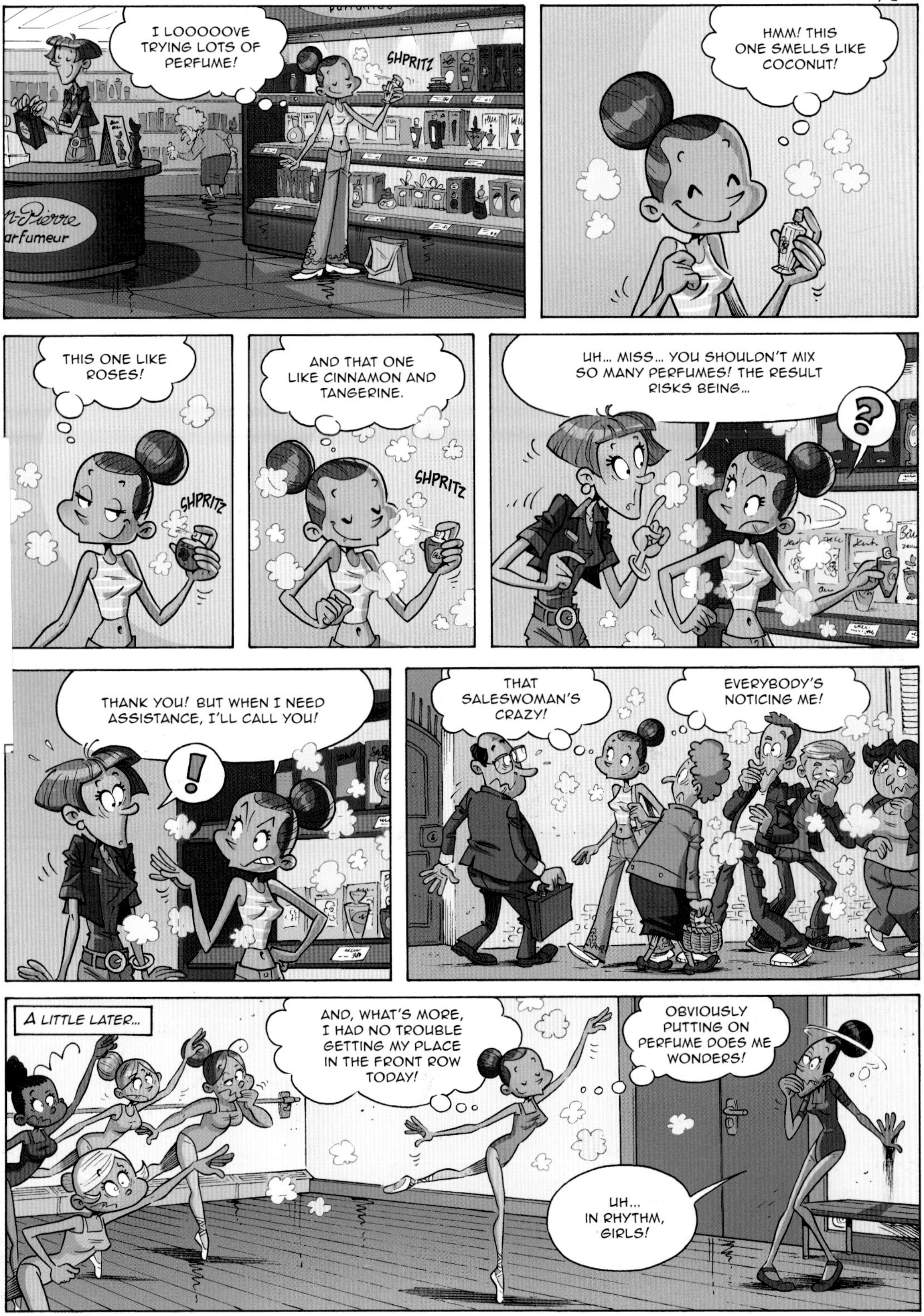
I LOOOOOVE TRYING LOTS OF PERFUME!
SHPRITZ
HMM! THIS ONE SMELLS LIKE COCONUT!
THIS ONE LIKE ROSES!
SHPRITZ
AND THAT ONE LIKE CINNAMON AND TANGERINE.
SHPRITZ
UH... MISS... YOU SHOULDN'T MIX SO MANY PERFUMES! THE RESULT RISKS BEING...
?
THANK YOU! BUT WHEN I NEED ASSISTANCE, I'LL CALL YOU!
!
THAT SALESWOMAN'S CRAZY!
EVERYBODY'S NOTICING ME!
A LITTLE LATER...
AND, WHAT'S MORE, I HAD NO TROUBLE GETTING MY PLACE IN THE FRONT ROW TODAY!
OBVIOUSLY PUTTING ON PERFUME DOES ME WONDERS!
UH... IN RHYTHM, GIRLS!

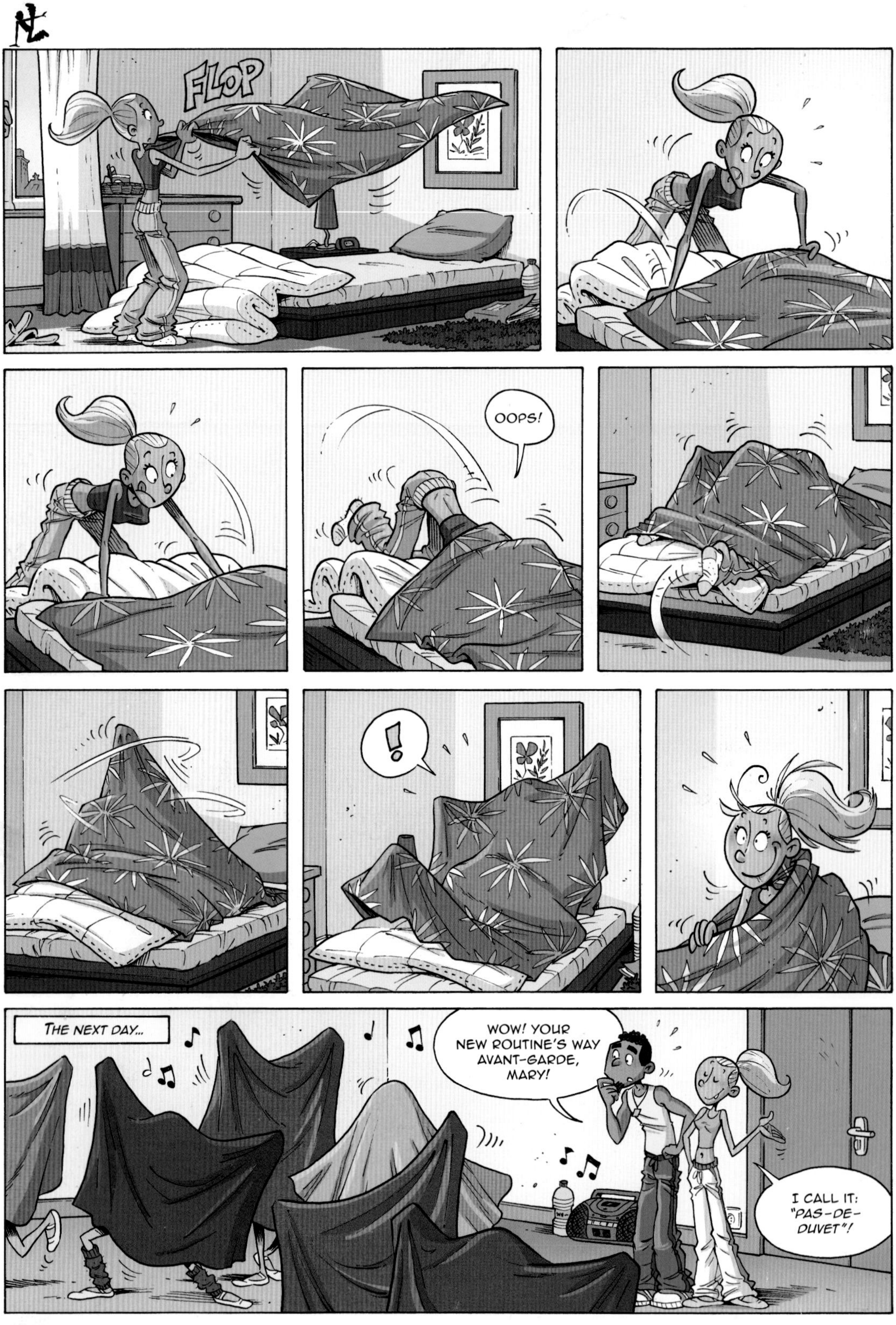
FLOP
OOPS!
!
THE NEXT DAY...
WOW! YOUR NEW ROUTINE'S WAY AVANT-GARDE, MARY!
I CALL IT: "PAS-DE-DUVET"!

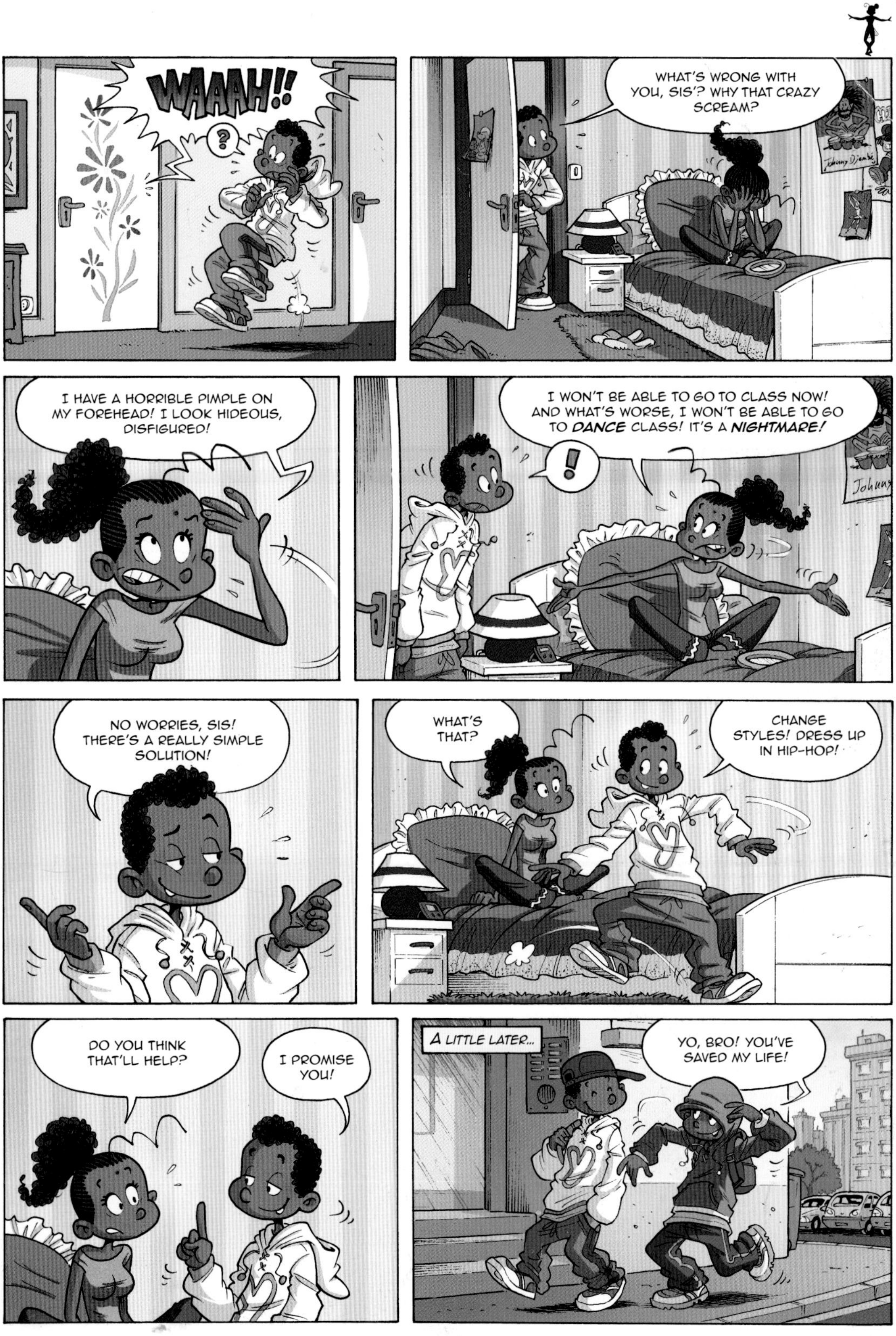
WAAAH!!
?
WHAT'S WRONG WITH YOU, SIS'? WHY THAT CRAZY SCREAM?
Johnny Djembé
I HAVE A HORRIBLE PIMPLE ON MY FOREHEAD! I LOOK HIDEOUS, DISFIGURED!
I WON'T BE ABLE TO GO TO CLASS NOW! AND WHAT'S WORSE, I WON'T BE ABLE TO GO TO DANCE CLASS! IT'S A NIGHTMARE!
!
NO WORRIES, SIS! THERE'S A REALLY SIMPLE SOLUTION!
WHAT'S THAT?
CHANGE STYLES! DRESS UP IN HIP-HOP!
DO YOU THINK THAT'LL HELP?
I PROMISE YOU!
A LITTLE LATER...
YO, BRO! YOU'VE SAVED MY LIFE!

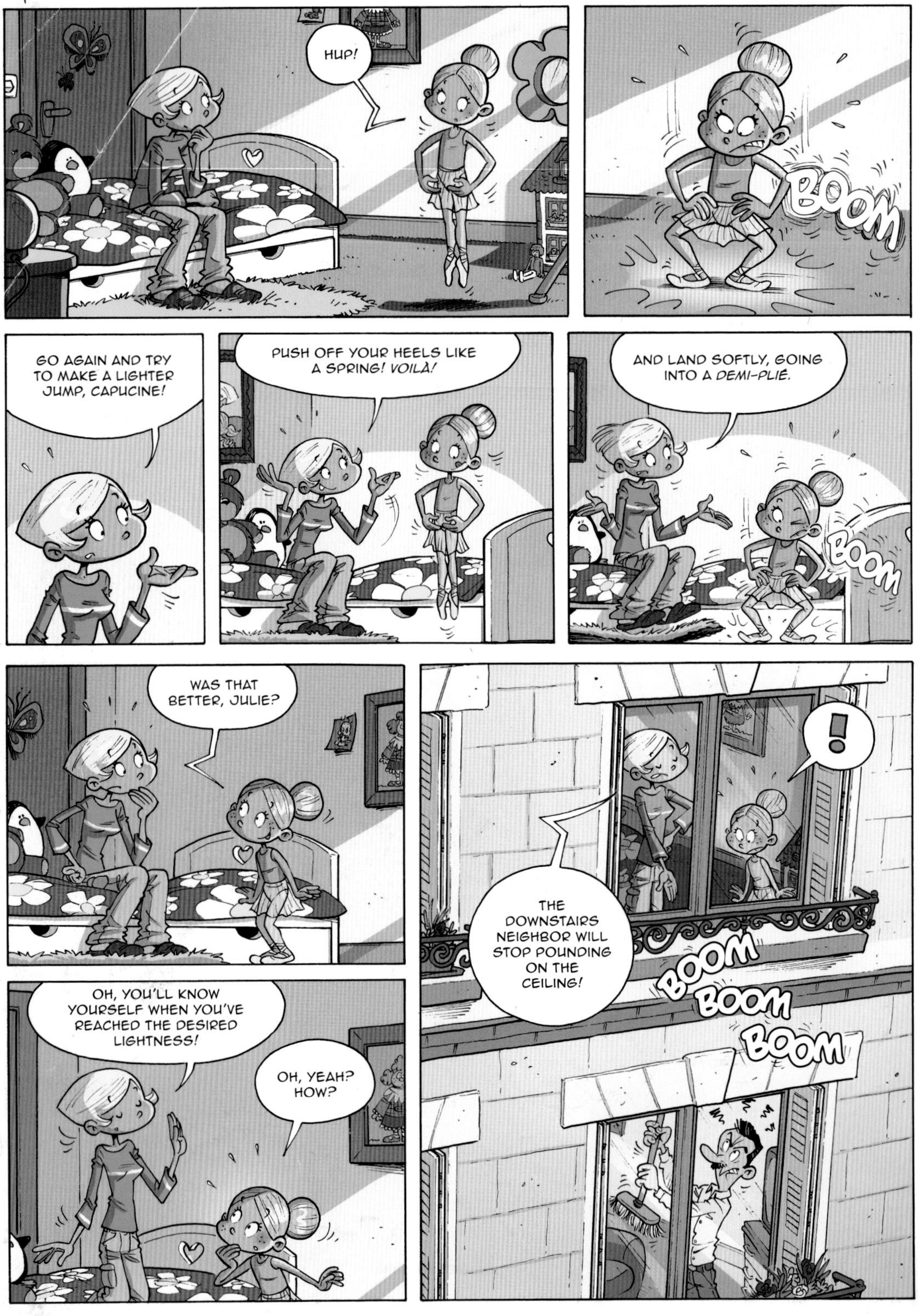
HUP!
BOOM
GO AGAIN AND TRY TO MAKE A LIGHTER JUMP, CAPUCINE!
PUSH OFF YOUR HEELS LIKE A SPRING! *VOILÀ!*
AND LAND SOFTLY, GOING INTO A *DEMI-PLIÉ*.
BOOM
WAS THAT BETTER, JULIE?
OH, YOU'LL KNOW YOURSELF WHEN YOU'VE REACHED THE DESIRED LIGHTNESS!
OH, YEAH? HOW?
!
THE DOWNSTAIRS NEIGHBOR WILL STOP POUNDING ON THE CEILING!
BOOM
BOOM
BOOM

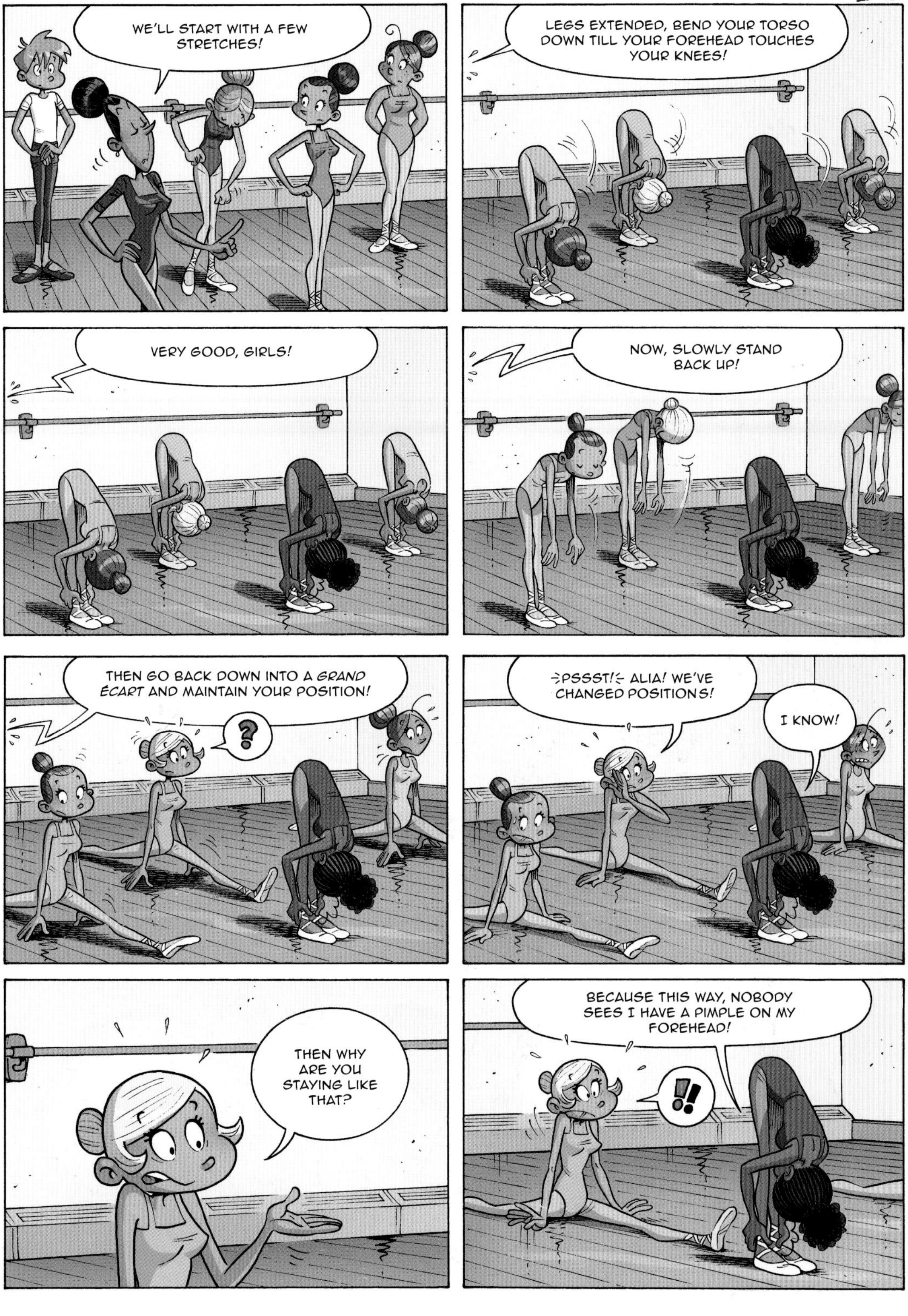
WE'LL START WITH A FEW STRETCHES!
LEGS EXTENDED, BEND YOUR TORSO DOWN TILL YOUR FOREHEAD TOUCHES YOUR KNEES!
VERY GOOD, GIRLS!
NOW, SLOWLY STAND BACK UP!
THEN GO BACK DOWN INTO A *GRAND ÉCART* AND MAINTAIN YOUR POSITION!
?
PSSST! ALIA! WE'VE CHANGED POSITIONS!
I KNOW!
THEN WHY ARE YOU STAYING LIKE THAT?
BECAUSE THIS WAY, NOBODY SEES I HAVE A PIMPLE ON MY FOREHEAD!
!!

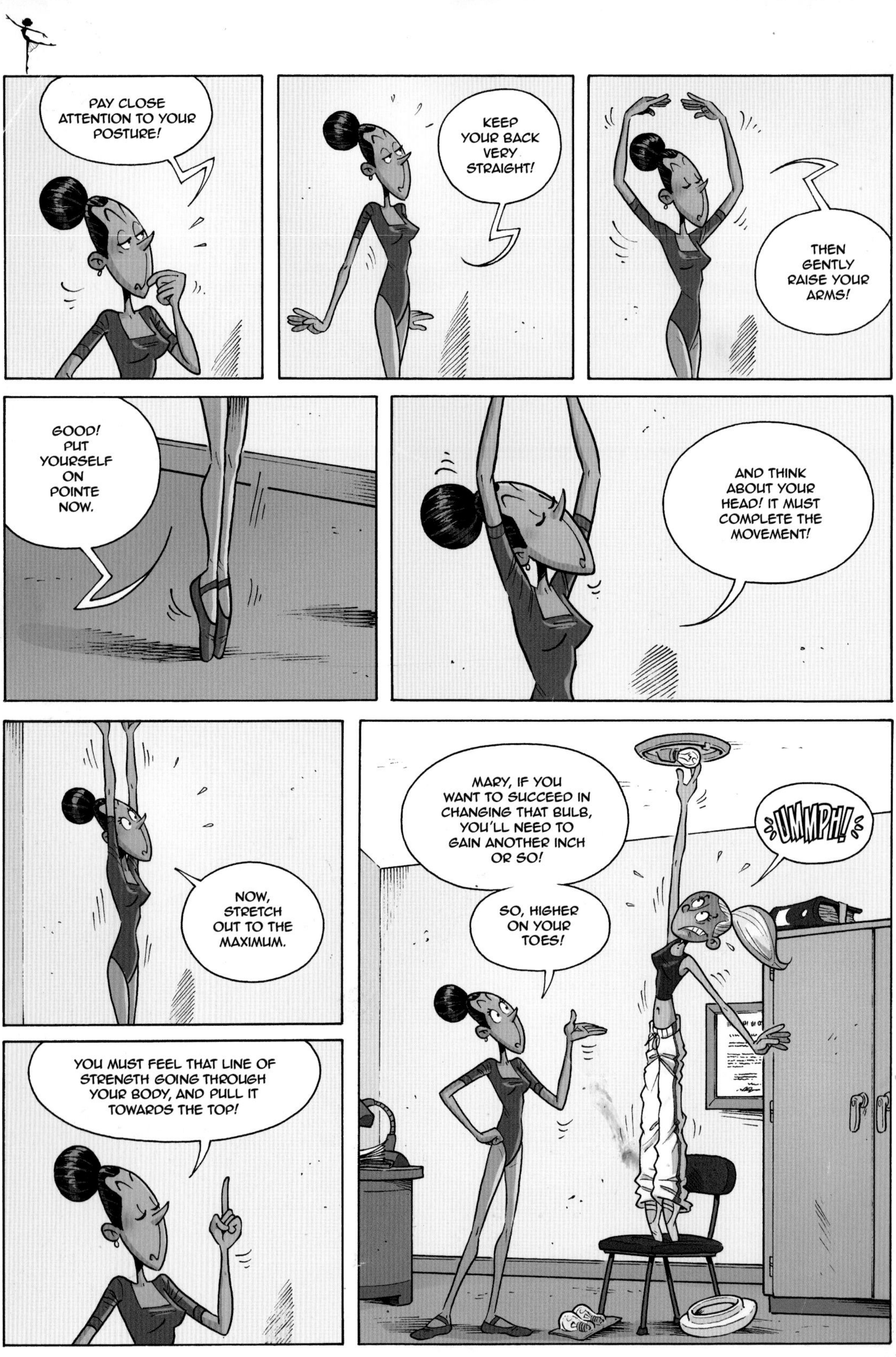
PAY CLOSE ATTENTION TO YOUR POSTURE!
KEEP YOUR BACK VERY STRAIGHT!
THEN GENTLY RAISE YOUR ARMS!
GOOD! PUT YOURSELF ON POINTE NOW.
AND THINK ABOUT YOUR HEAD! IT MUST COMPLETE THE MOVEMENT!
NOW, STRETCH OUT TO THE MAXIMUM.
YOU MUST FEEL THAT LINE OF STRENGTH GOING THROUGH YOUR BODY, AND PULL IT TOWARDS THE TOP!
MARY, IF YOU WANT TO SUCCEED IN CHANGING THAT BULB, YOU'LL NEED TO GAIN ANOTHER INCH OR SO!
SO, HIGHER ON YOUR TOES!
UMMPH!

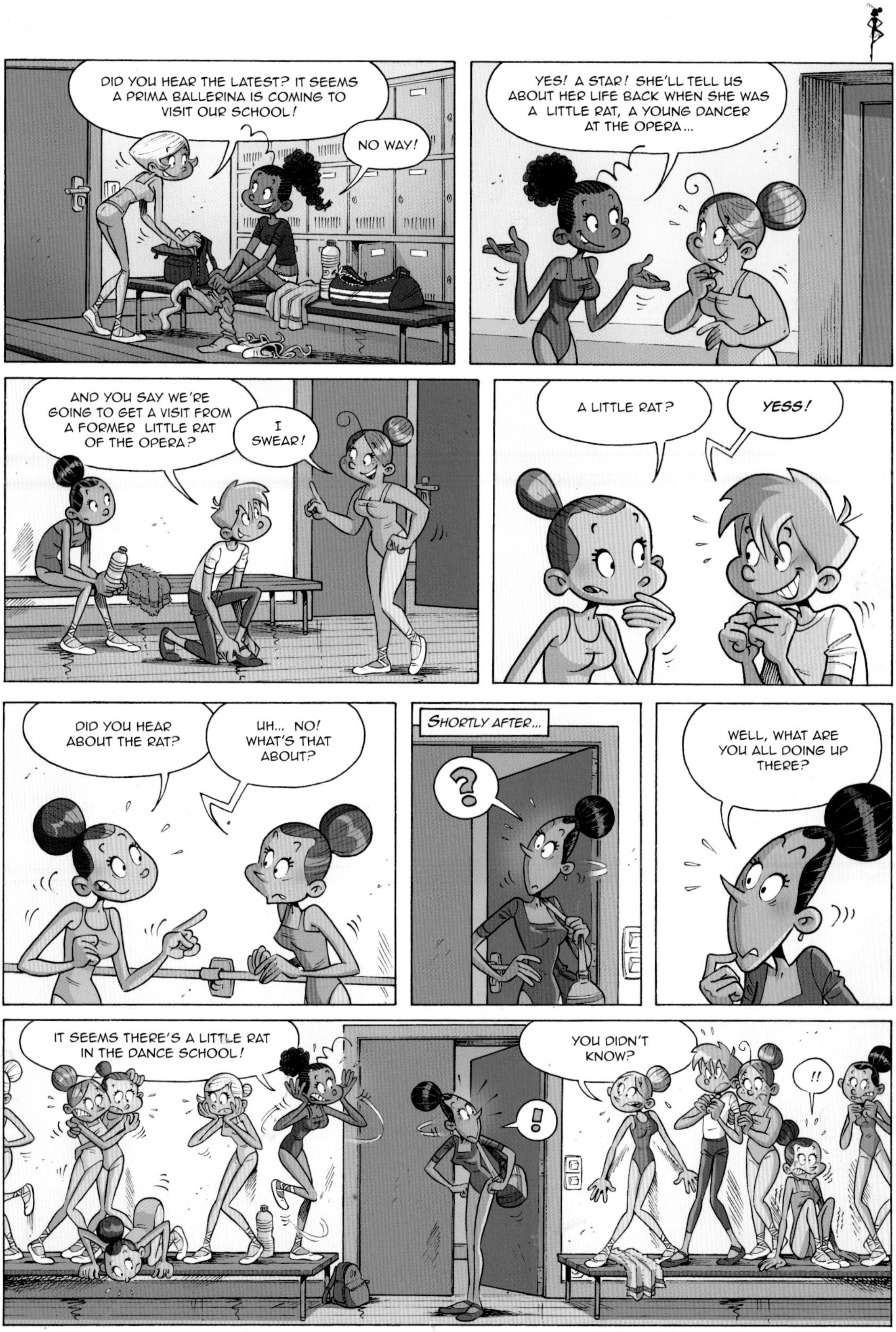

DID YOU HEAR THE LATEST? IT SEEMS A PRIMA BALLERINA IS COMING TO VISIT OUR SCHOOL!
NO WAY!
YES! A STAR! SHE'LL TELL US ABOUT HER LIFE BACK WHEN SHE WAS A LITTLE RAT, A YOUNG DANCER AT THE OPERA...
AND YOU SAY WE'RE GOING TO GET A VISIT FROM A FORMER LITTLE RAT OF THE OPERA?
I SWEAR!
A LITTLE RAT?
YESS!
DID YOU HEAR ABOUT THE RAT?
UH... NO! WHAT'S THAT ABOUT?
SHORTLY AFTER...
?
WELL, WHAT ARE YOU ALL DOING UP THERE?
IT SEEMS THERE'S A LITTLE RAT IN THE DANCE SCHOOL!
!
YOU DIDN'T KNOW?
!!

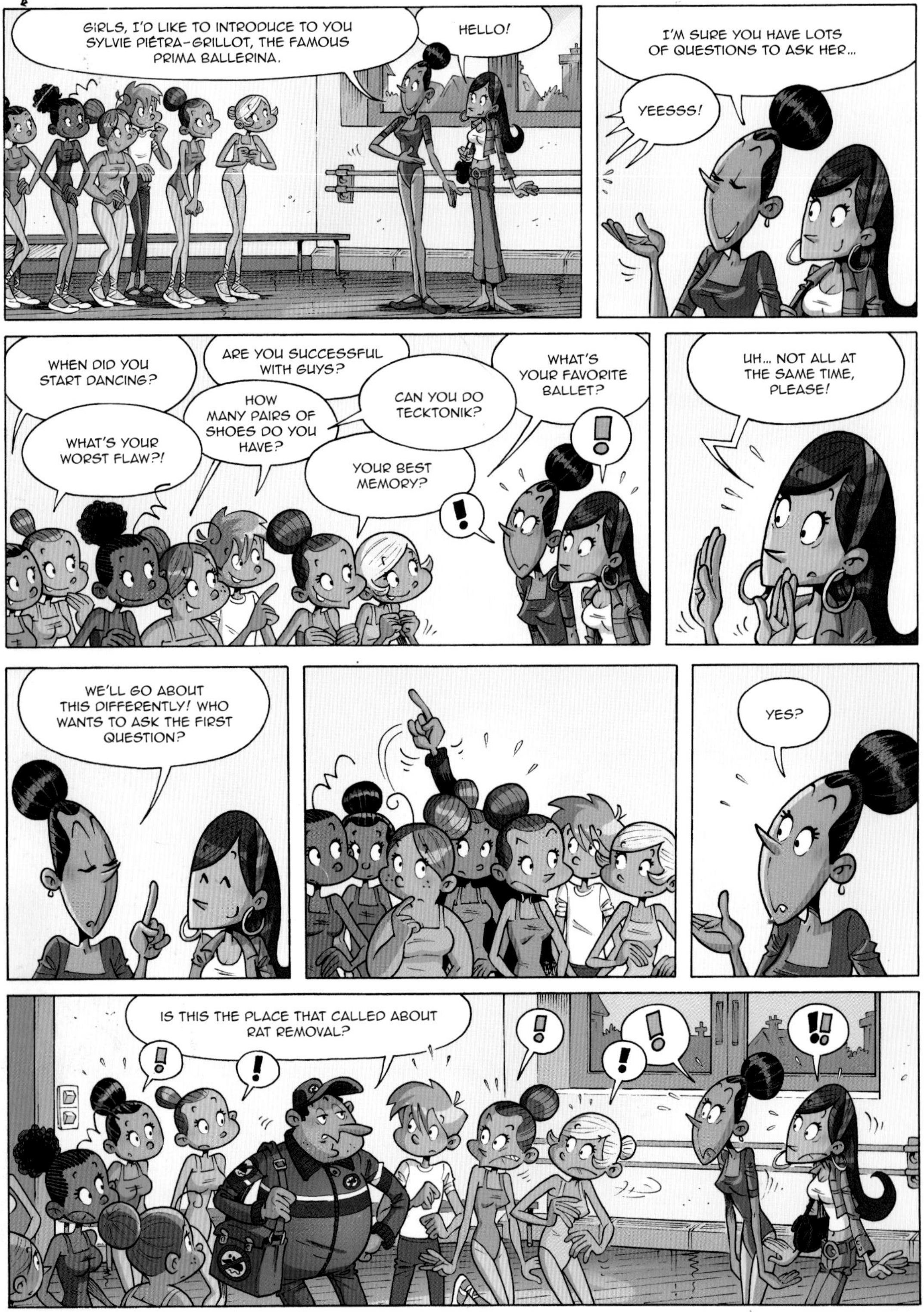
GIRLS, I'D LIKE TO INTRODUCE TO YOU SYLVIE PIÉTRA-GRILLOT, THE FAMOUS PRIMA BALLERINA.
HELLO!
I'M SURE YOU HAVE LOTS OF QUESTIONS TO ASK HER...
YEESSS!
WHEN DID YOU START DANCING?
ARE YOU SUCCESSFUL WITH GUYS?
WHAT'S YOUR FAVORITE BALLET?
HOW MANY PAIRS OF SHOES DO YOU HAVE?
CAN YOU DO TECKTONIK?
WHAT'S YOUR WORST FLAW?!
YOUR BEST MEMORY?
!
!
UH... NOT ALL AT THE SAME TIME, PLEASE!
WE'LL GO ABOUT THIS DIFFERENTLY! WHO WANTS TO ASK THE FIRST QUESTION?
YES?
IS THIS THE PLACE THAT CALLED ABOUT RAT REMOVAL?
!
!
!
!
!
!!

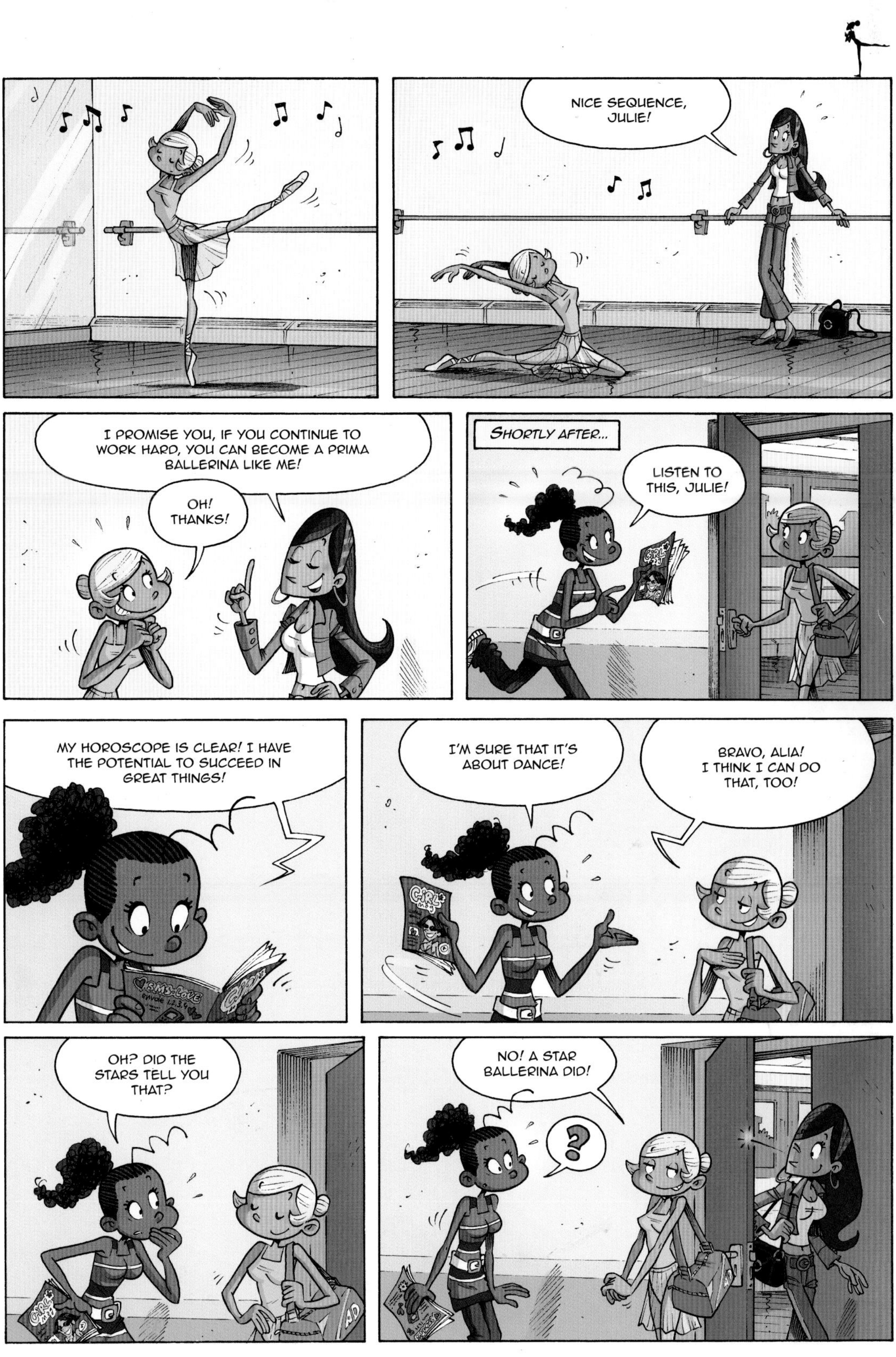
NICE SEQUENCE, JULIE!
I PROMISE YOU, IF YOU CONTINUE TO WORK HARD, YOU CAN BECOME A PRIMA BALLERINA LIKE ME!
OH! THANKS!
SHORTLY AFTER...
LISTEN TO THIS, JULIE!
MY HOROSCOPE IS CLEAR! I HAVE THE POTENTIAL TO SUCCEED IN GREAT THINGS!
I'M SURE THAT IT'S ABOUT DANCE!
BRAVO, ALIA! I THINK I CAN DO THAT, TOO!
OH? DID THE STARS TELL YOU THAT?
NO! A STAR BALLERINA DID!
?

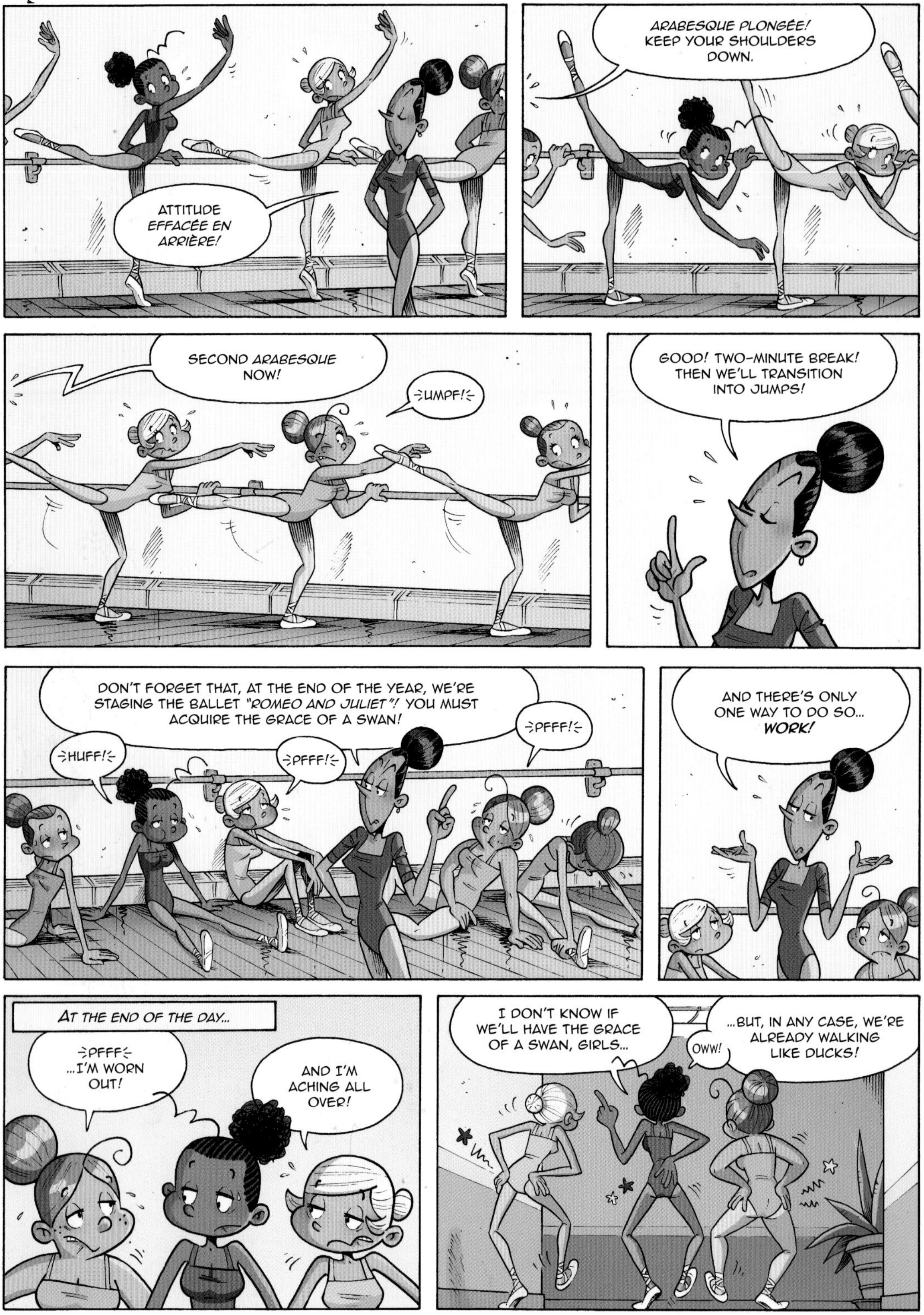
ATTITUDE EFFACÉE EN ARRIÈRE!
ARABESQUE PLONGÉE! KEEP YOUR SHOULDERS DOWN.
SECOND ARABESQUE NOW!
UMPF!
GOOD! TWO-MINUTE BREAK! THEN WE'LL TRANSITION INTO JUMPS!
DON'T FORGET THAT, AT THE END OF THE YEAR, WE'RE STAGING THE BALLET "ROMEO AND JULIET"! YOU MUST ACQUIRE THE GRACE OF A SWAN!
HUFF!
PFFF!
PFFF!
AND THERE'S ONLY ONE WAY TO DO SO... WORK!
AT THE END OF THE DAY...
PFFF ...I'M WORN OUT!
AND I'M ACHING ALL OVER!
I DON'T KNOW IF WE'LL HAVE THE GRACE OF A SWAN, GIRLS...
OWW!
...BUT, IN ANY CASE, WE'RE ALREADY WALKING LIKE DUCKS!

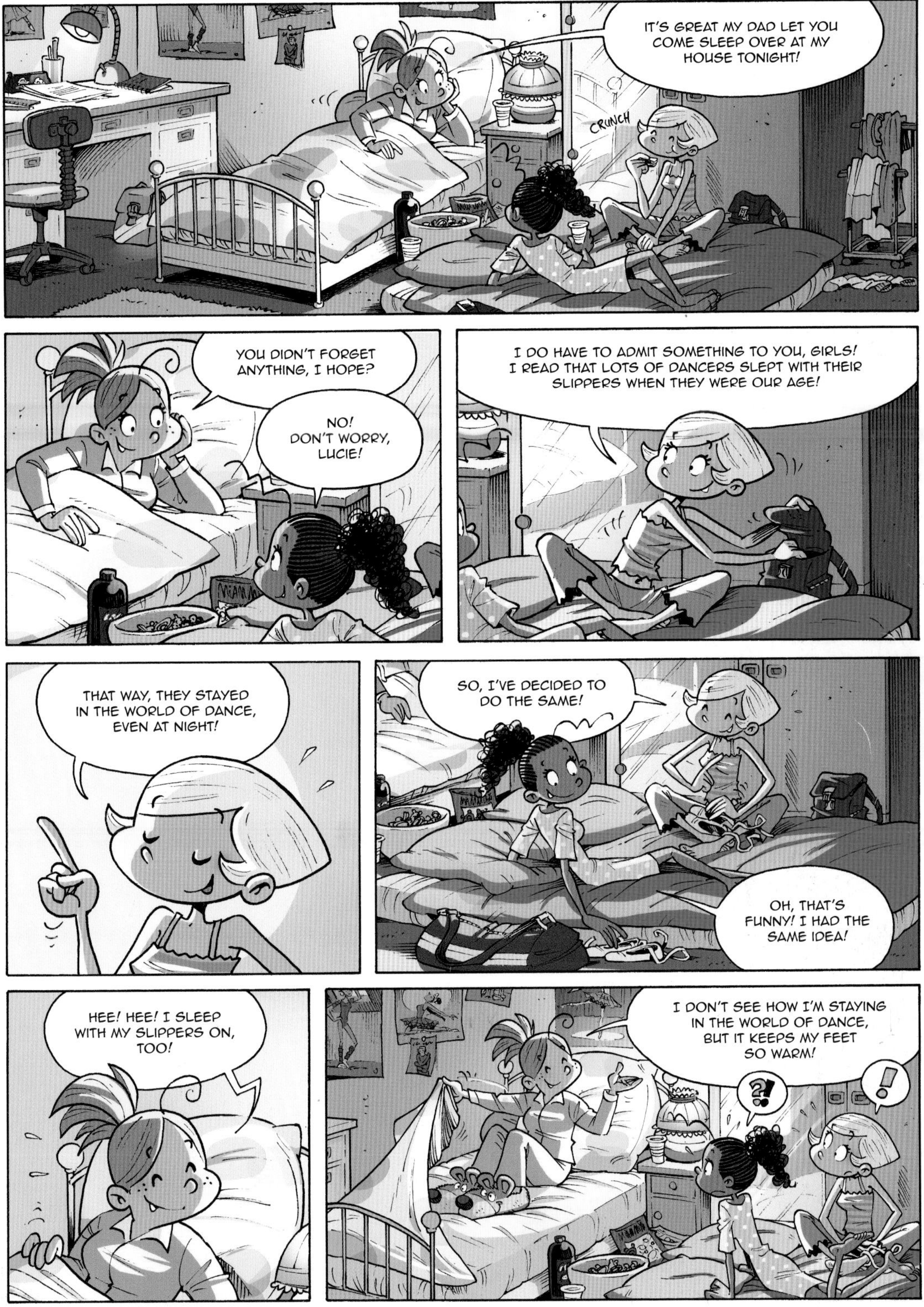
IT'S GREAT MY DAD LET YOU COME SLEEP OVER AT MY HOUSE TONIGHT!
CRUNCH
YOU DIDN'T FORGET ANYTHING, I HOPE?
NO! DON'T WORRY, LUCIE!
I DO HAVE TO ADMIT SOMETHING TO YOU, GIRLS! I READ THAT LOTS OF DANCERS SLEPT WITH THEIR SLIPPERS WHEN THEY WERE OUR AGE!
THAT WAY, THEY STAYED IN THE WORLD OF DANCE, EVEN AT NIGHT!
SO, I'VE DECIDED TO DO THE SAME!
OH, THAT'S FUNNY! I HAD THE SAME IDEA!
HEE! HEE! I SLEEP WITH MY SLIPPERS ON, TOO!
I DON'T SEE HOW I'M STAYING IN THE WORLD OF DANCE, BUT IT KEEPS MY FEET SO WARM!
?!
!

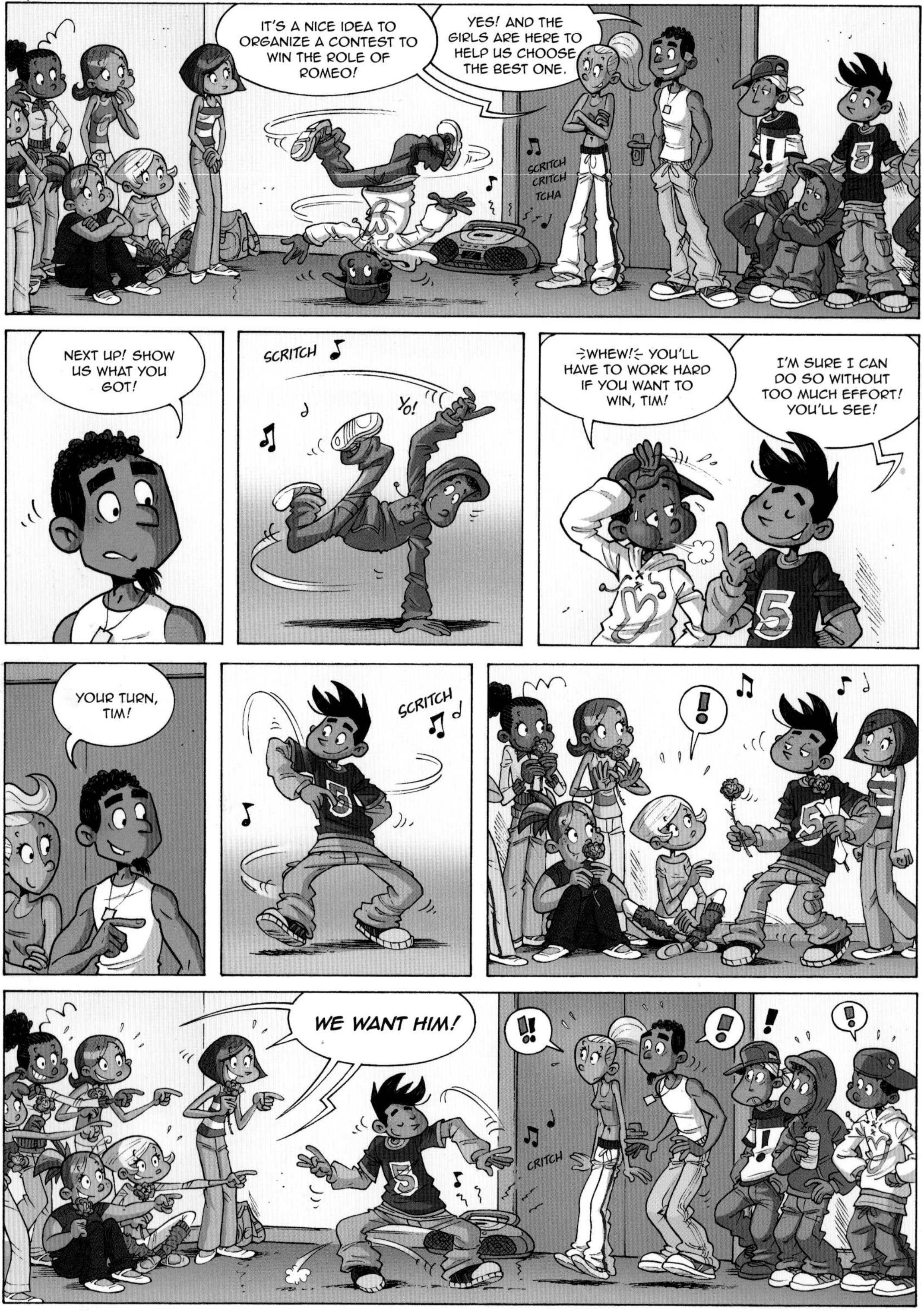

IT'S A NICE IDEA TO ORGANIZE A CONTEST TO WIN THE ROLE OF ROMEO!
YES! AND THE GIRLS ARE HERE TO HELP US CHOOSE THE BEST ONE.
SCRITCH CRITCH TCHA
NEXT UP! SHOW US WHAT YOU GOT!
SCRITCH
YO!
-WHEW!- YOU'LL HAVE TO WORK HARD IF YOU WANT TO WIN, TIM!
I'M SURE I CAN DO SO WITHOUT TOO MUCH EFFORT! YOU'LL SEE!
YOUR TURN, TIM!
SCRITCH
!
WE WANT HIM!
!!
CRITCH
!
!
!

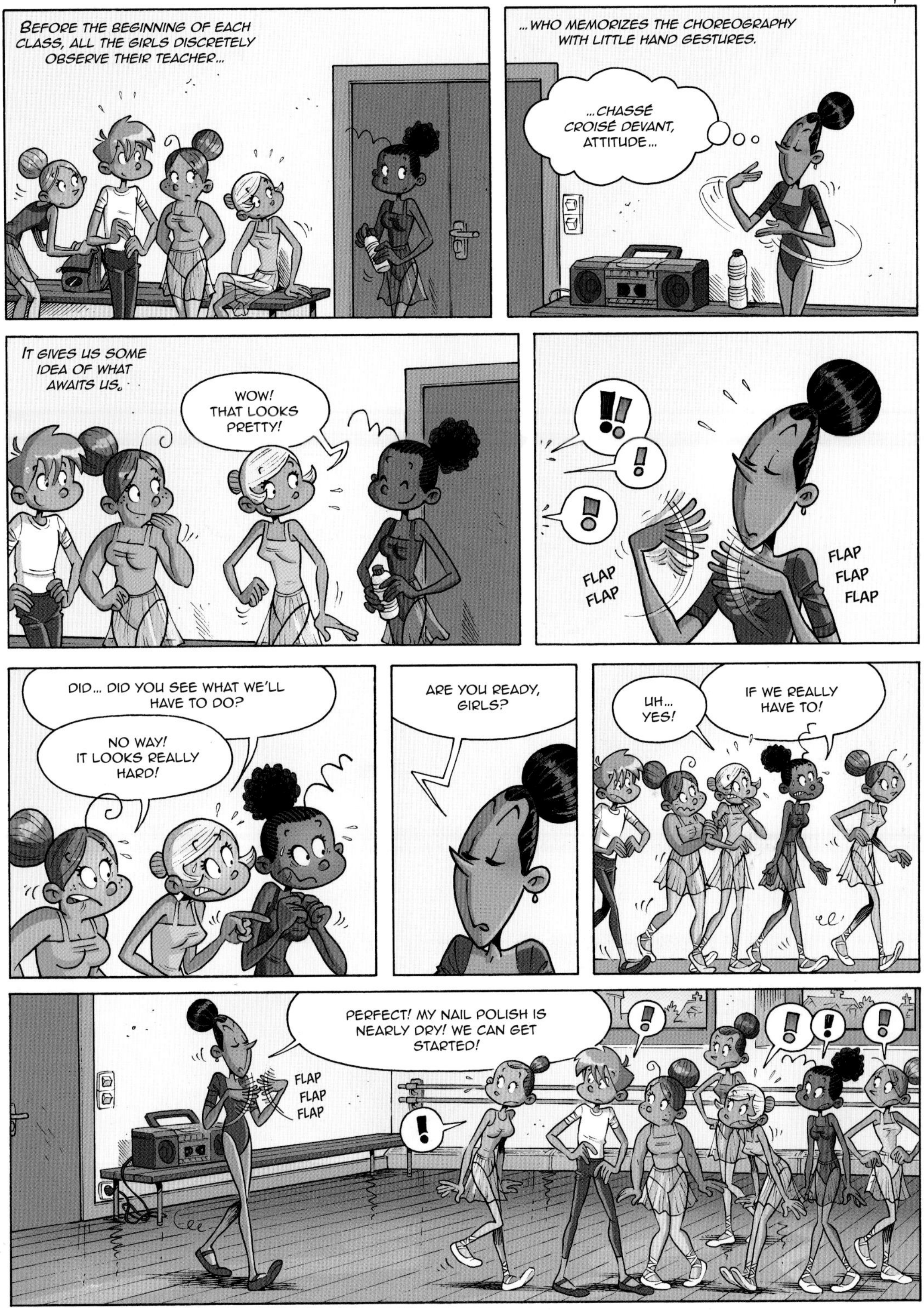
Before the beginning of each class, all the girls discretely observe their teacher...
...who memorizes the choreography with little hand gestures.
...chassé croisé devant, attitude...
It gives us some idea of what awaits us.
WOW! THAT LOOKS PRETTY!
!!
!
!
FLAP FLAP
FLAP FLAP FLAP
DID... DID YOU SEE WHAT WE'LL HAVE TO DO?
NO WAY! IT LOOKS REALLY HARD!
ARE YOU READY, GIRLS?
UH... YES!
IF WE REALLY HAVE TO!
PERFECT! MY NAIL POLISH IS NEARLY DRY! WE CAN GET STARTED!
FLAP FLAP FLAP
!
!
!
!
!

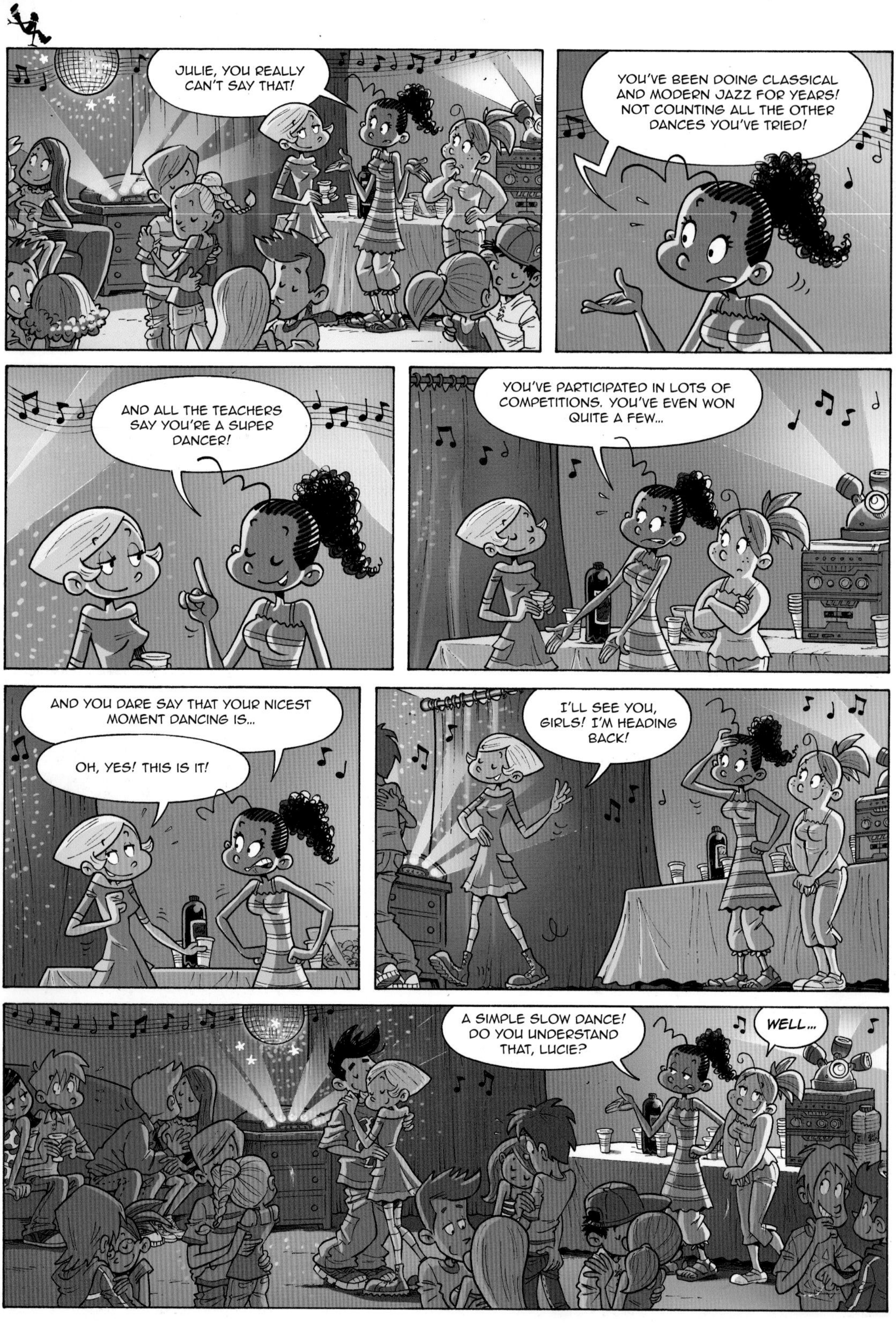
JULIE, YOU REALLY CAN'T SAY THAT!
YOU'VE BEEN DOING CLASSICAL AND MODERN JAZZ FOR YEARS! NOT COUNTING ALL THE OTHER DANCES YOU'VE TRIED!
AND ALL THE TEACHERS SAY YOU'RE A SUPER DANCER!
YOU'VE PARTICIPATED IN LOTS OF COMPETITIONS. YOU'VE EVEN WON QUITE A FEW...
AND YOU DARE SAY THAT YOUR NICEST MOMENT DANCING IS...
OH, YES! THIS IS IT!
I'LL SEE YOU, GIRLS! I'M HEADING BACK!
A SIMPLE SLOW DANCE! DO YOU UNDERSTAND THAT, LUCIE?
WELL...

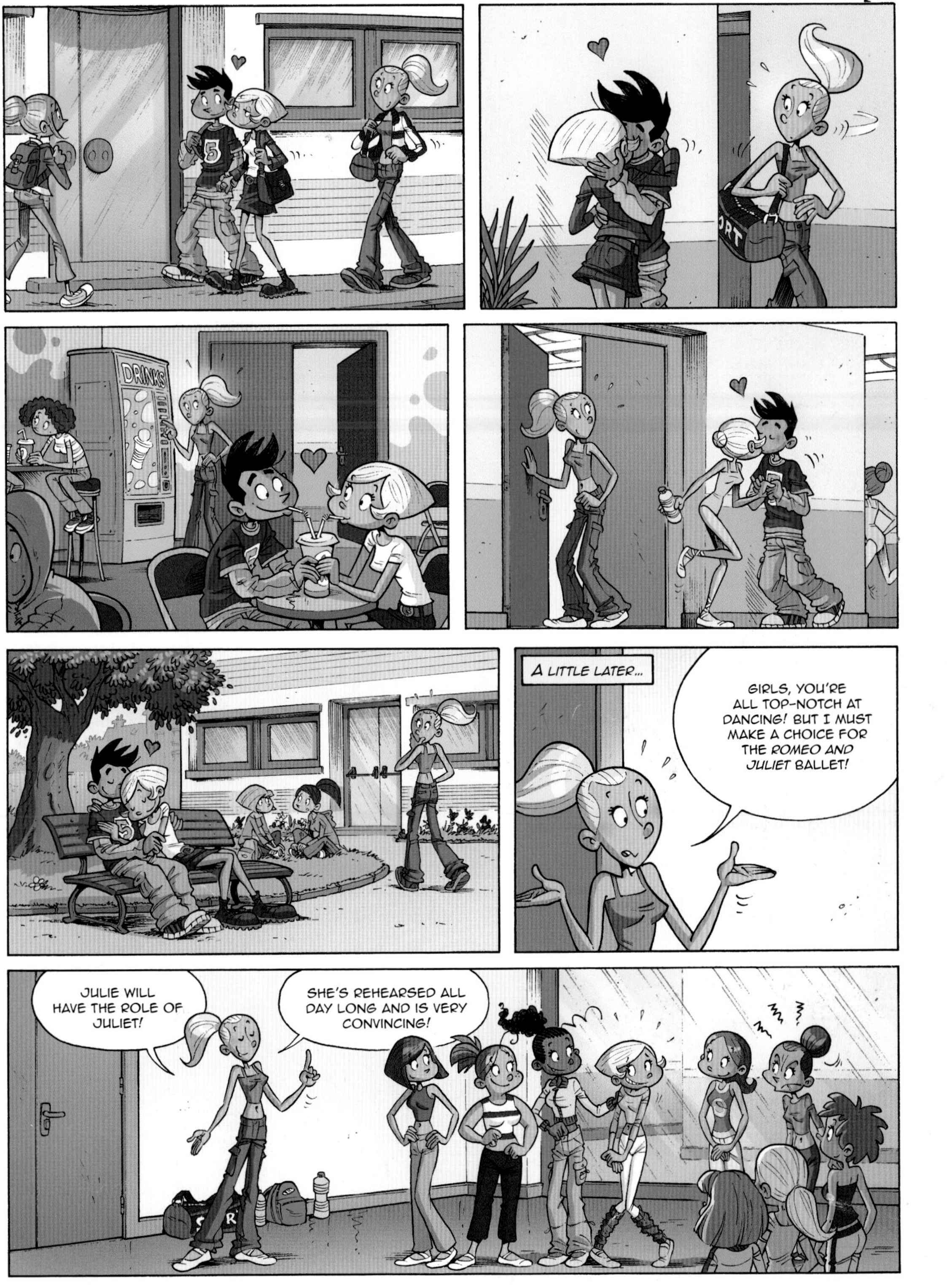
DRINKS
A LITTLE LATER...
GIRLS, YOU'RE ALL TOP-NOTCH AT DANCING! BUT I MUST MAKE A CHOICE FOR THE *ROMEO AND JULIET* BALLET!
JULIE WILL HAVE THE ROLE OF JULIET!
SHE'S REHEARSED ALL DAY LONG AND IS VERY CONVINCING!

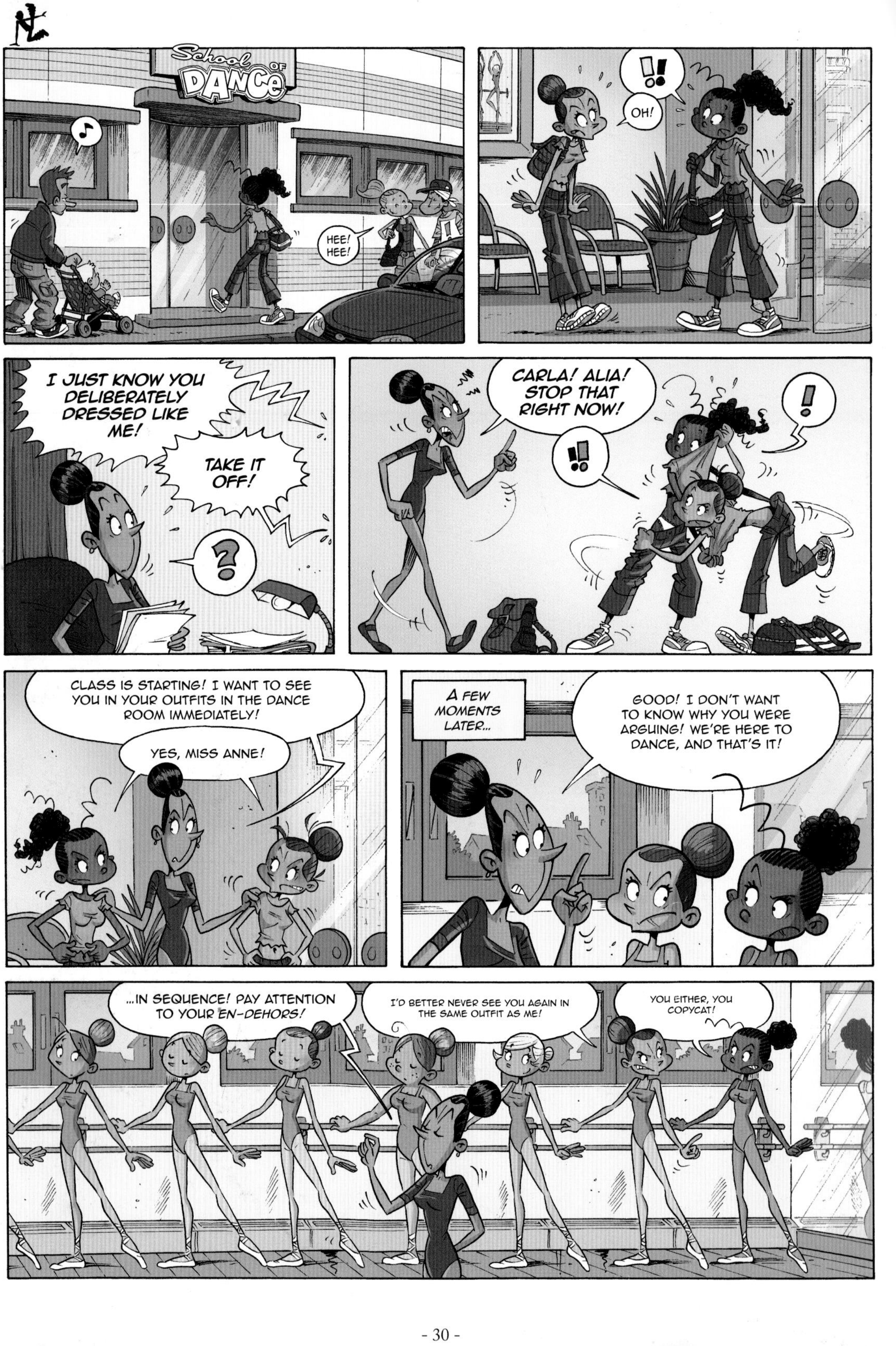
School of DANCE
HEE! HEE!
OH!
I JUST KNOW YOU DELIBERATELY DRESSED LIKE ME!
TAKE IT OFF!
?
CARLA! ALIA! STOP THAT RIGHT NOW!
!
CLASS IS STARTING! I WANT TO SEE YOU IN YOUR OUTFITS IN THE DANCE ROOM IMMEDIATELY!
YES, MISS ANNE!
A FEW MOMENTS LATER...
GOOD! I DON'T WANT TO KNOW WHY YOU WERE ARGUING! WE'RE HERE TO DANCE, AND THAT'S IT!
...IN SEQUENCE! PAY ATTENTION TO YOUR EN-DEHORS!
I'D BETTER NEVER SEE YOU AGAIN IN THE SAME OUTFIT AS ME!
YOU EITHER, YOU COPYCAT!

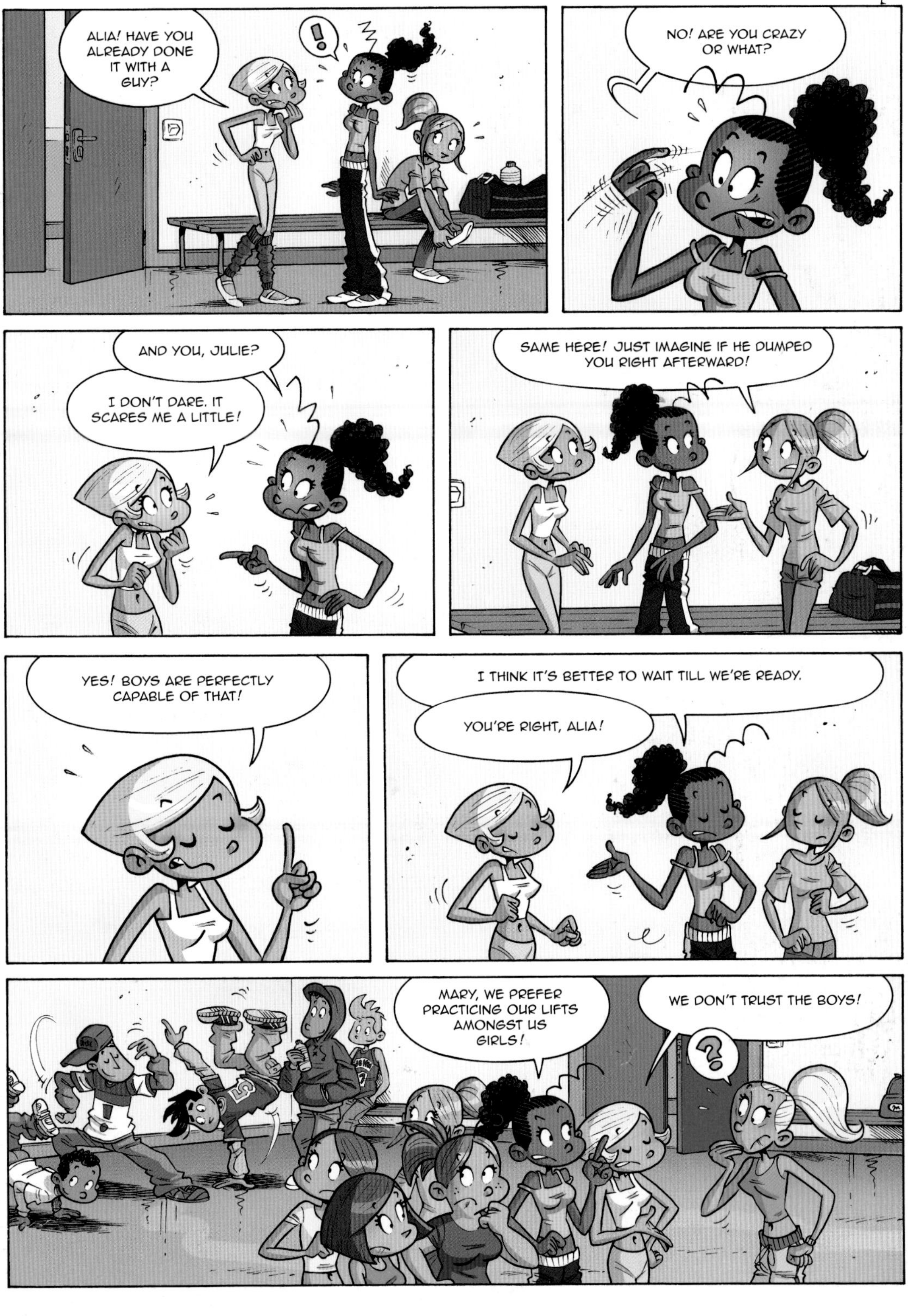
ALIA! HAVE YOU ALREADY DONE IT WITH A GUY?
!
NO! ARE YOU CRAZY OR WHAT?
AND YOU, JULIE?
I DON'T DARE. IT SCARES ME A LITTLE!
SAME HERE! JUST IMAGINE IF HE DUMPED YOU RIGHT AFTERWARD!
YES! BOYS ARE PERFECTLY CAPABLE OF THAT!
I THINK IT'S BETTER TO WAIT TILL WE'RE READY.
YOU'RE RIGHT, ALIA!
MARY, WE PREFER PRACTICING OUR LIFTS AMONGST US GIRLS!
WE DON'T TRUST THE BOYS!
?

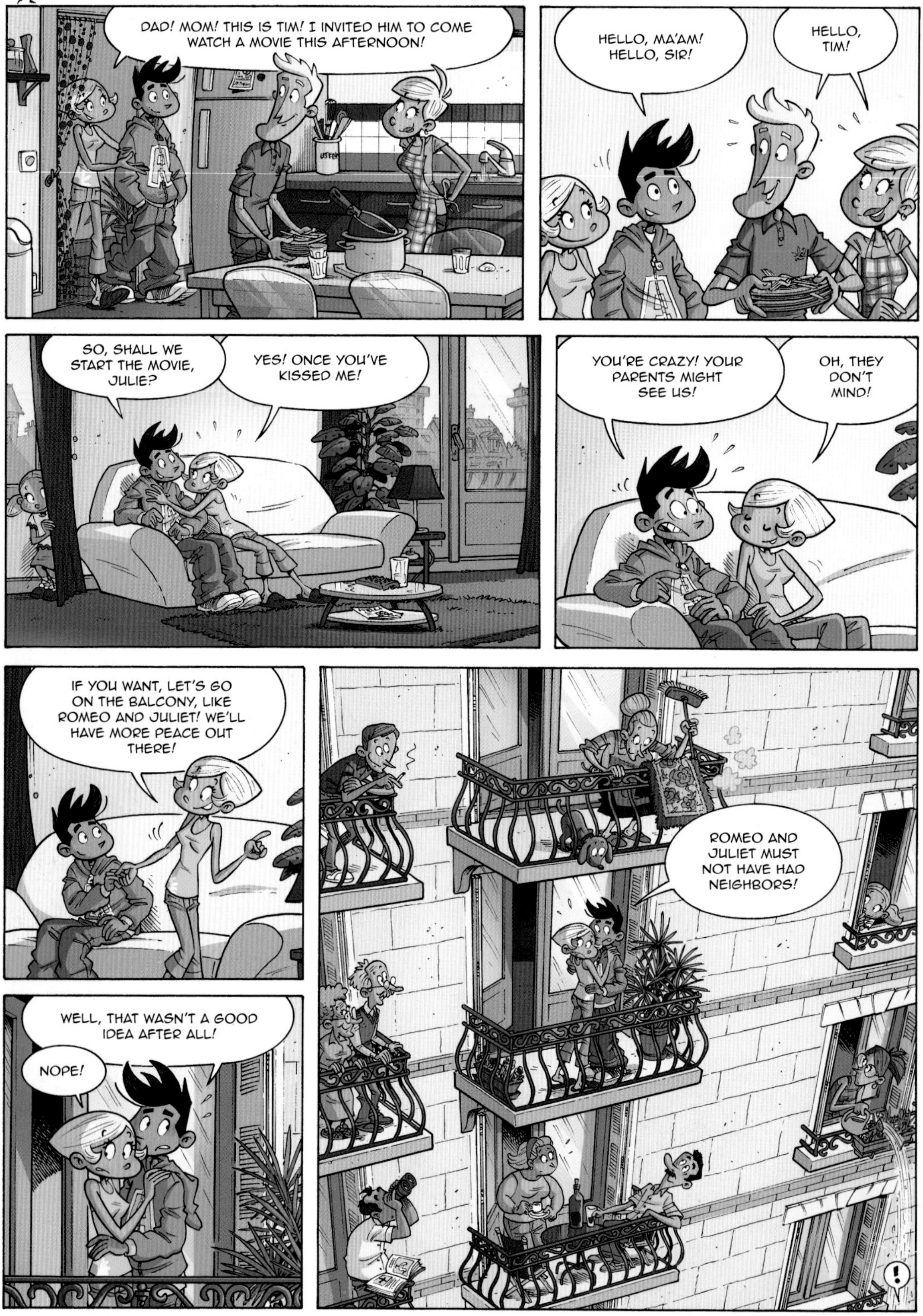
DAD! MOM! THIS IS TIM! I INVITED HIM TO COME WATCH A MOVIE THIS AFTERNOON!
HELLO, MA'AM! HELLO, SIR!
HELLO, TIM!
SO, SHALL WE START THE MOVIE, JULIE?
YES! ONCE YOU'VE KISSED ME!
YOU'RE CRAZY! YOUR PARENTS MIGHT SEE US!
OH, THEY DON'T MIND!
IF YOU WANT, LET'S GO ON THE BALCONY, LIKE ROMEO AND JULIET! WE'LL HAVE MORE PEACE OUT THERE!
WELL, THAT WASN'T A GOOD IDEA AFTER ALL!
NOPE!
ROMEO AND JULIET MUST NOT HAVE HAD NEIGHBORS!
!

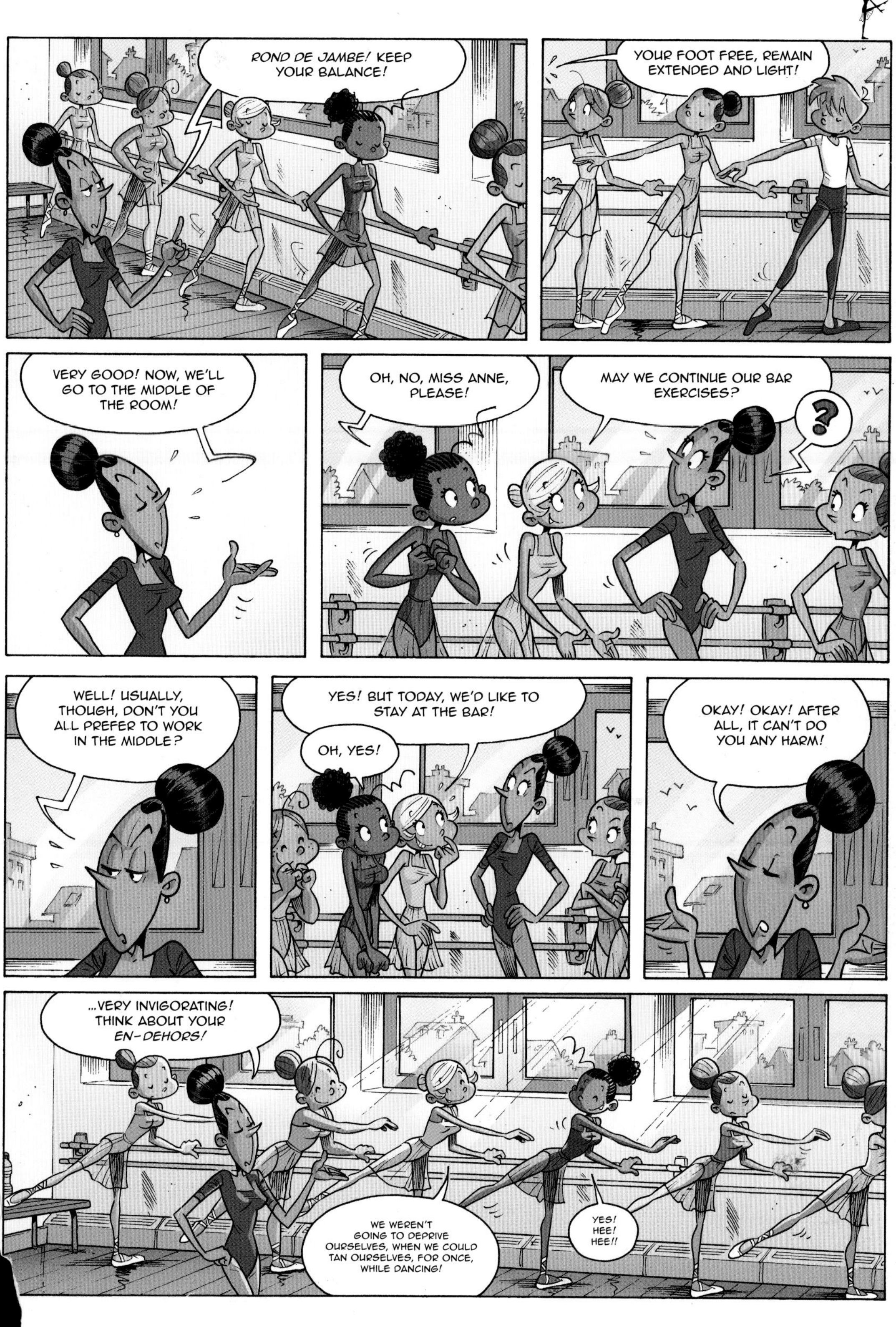
RONDE DE JAMBE! KEEP YOUR BALANCE!
YOUR FOOT FREE, REMAIN EXTENDED AND LIGHT!
VERY GOOD! NOW, WE'LL GO TO THE MIDDLE OF THE ROOM!
OH, NO, MISS ANNE, PLEASE!
MAY WE CONTINUE OUR BAR EXERCISES?
?
WELL! USUALLY, THOUGH, DON'T YOU ALL PREFER TO WORK IN THE MIDDLE?
YES! BUT TODAY, WE'D LIKE TO STAY AT THE BAR!
OH, YES!
OKAY! OKAY! AFTER ALL, IT CAN'T DO YOU ANY HARM!
...VERY INVIGORATING! THINK ABOUT YOUR EN-DEHORS!
WE WEREN'T GOING TO DEPRIVE OURSELVES, WHEN WE COULD TAN OURSELVES, FOR ONCE, WHILE DANCING!
YES! HEE! HEE!!

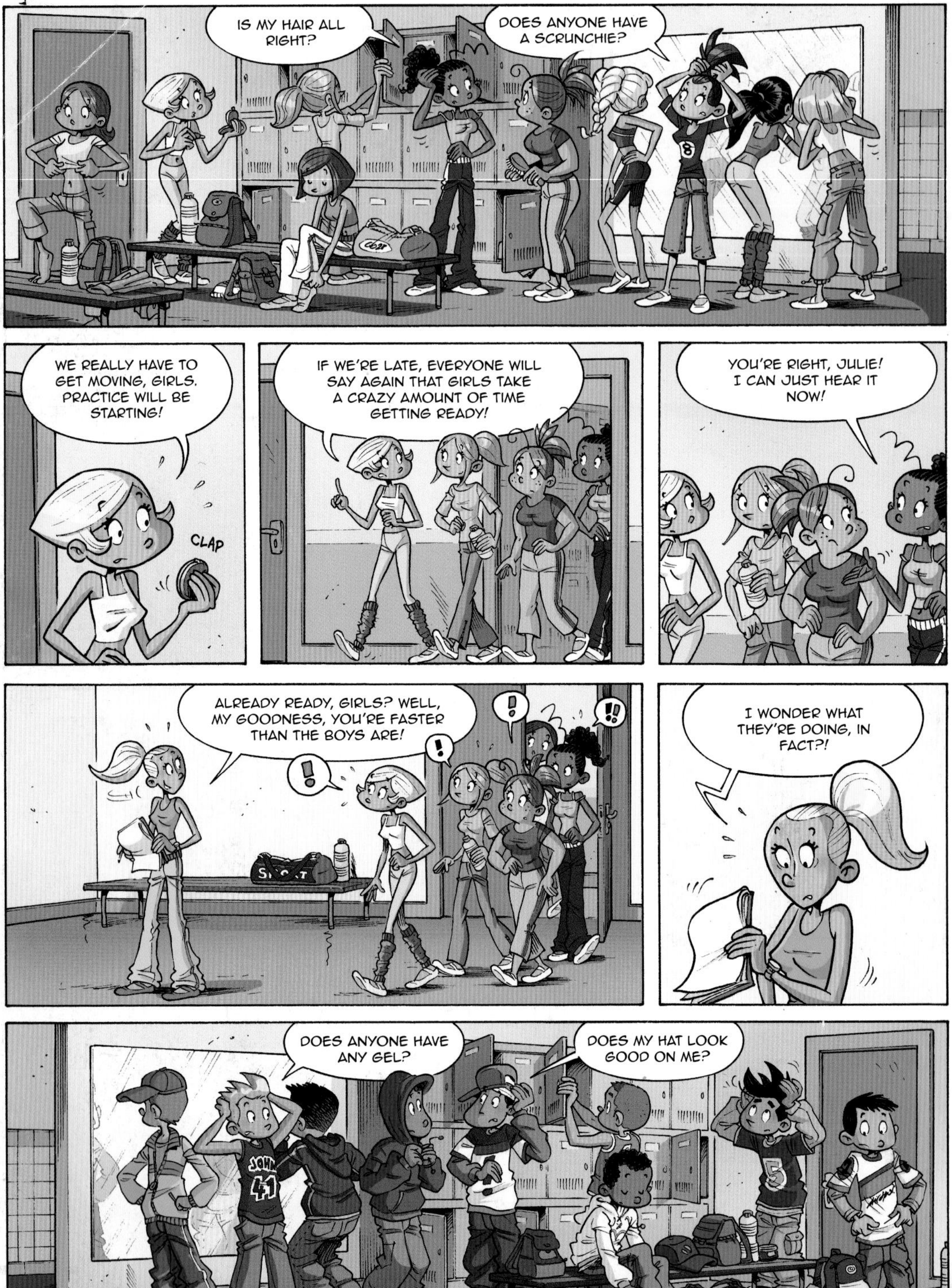
IS MY HAIR ALL RIGHT?
DOES ANYONE HAVE A SCRUNCHIE?
WE REALLY HAVE TO GET MOVING, GIRLS. PRACTICE WILL BE STARTING!
CLAP
IF WE'RE LATE, EVERYONE WILL SAY AGAIN THAT GIRLS TAKE A CRAZY AMOUNT OF TIME GETTING READY!
YOU'RE RIGHT, JULIE! I CAN JUST HEAR IT NOW!
ALREADY READY, GIRLS? WELL, MY GOODNESS, YOU'RE FASTER THAN THE BOYS ARE!
!
!
!
!!
I WONDER WHAT THEY'RE DOING, IN FACT?!
DOES ANYONE HAVE ANY GEL?
DOES MY HAT LOOK GOOD ON ME?

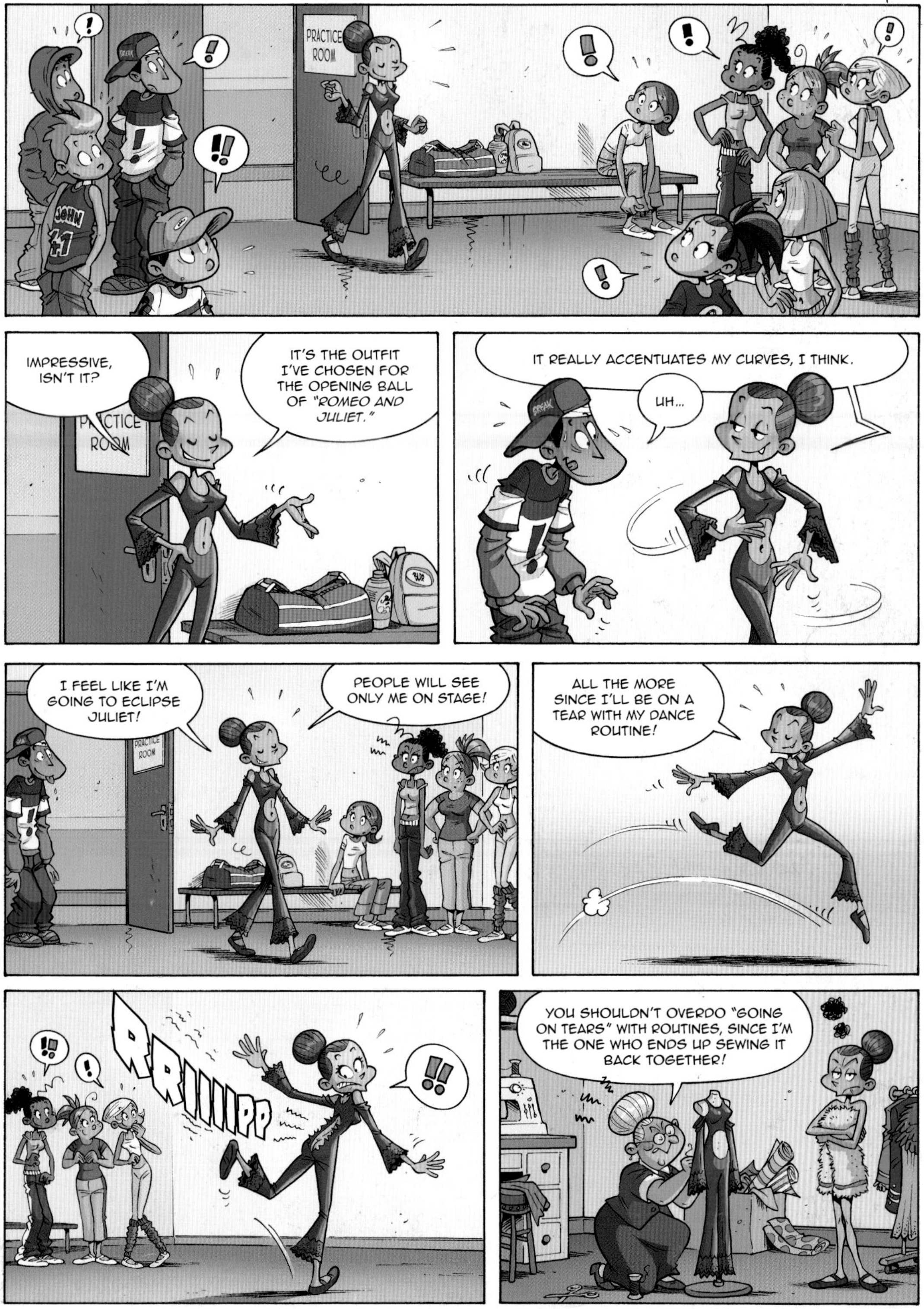

!
!
!!
!
!
!
!
PRACTICE ROOM
IMPRESSIVE, ISN'T IT?
IT'S THE OUTFIT I'VE CHOSEN FOR THE OPENING BALL OF "ROMEO AND JULIET."
IT REALLY ACCENTUATES MY CURVES, I THINK.
UH...
I FEEL LIKE I'M GOING TO ECLIPSE JULIET!
PEOPLE WILL SEE ONLY ME ON STAGE!
ALL THE MORE SINCE I'LL BE ON A TEAR WITH MY DANCE ROUTINE!
!!
!
RRIIIIIPP
!!
YOU SHOULDN'T OVERDO "GOING ON TEARS" WITH ROUTINES, SINCE I'M THE ONE WHO ENDS UP SEWING IT BACK TOGETHER!

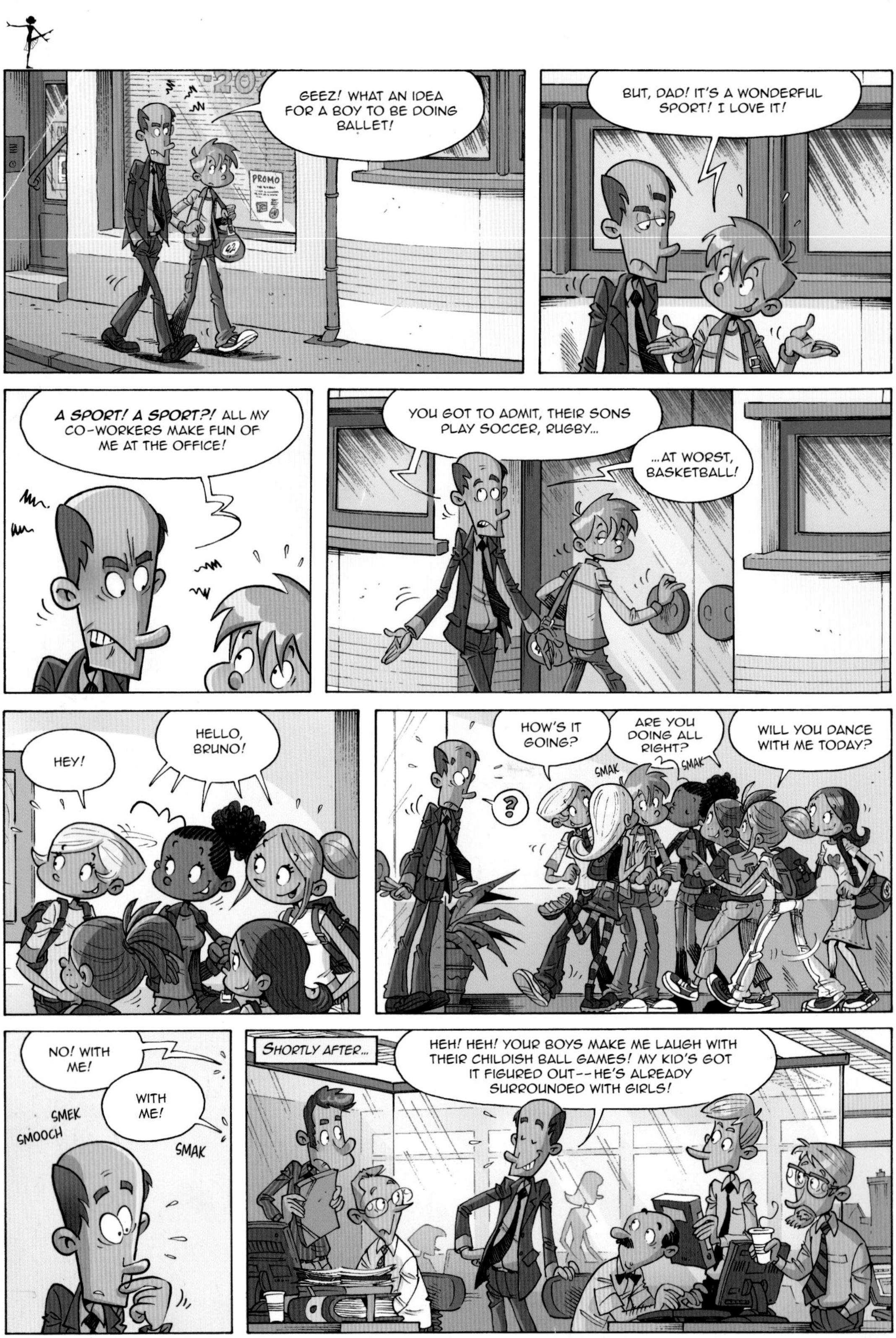
GEEZ! WHAT AN IDEA FOR A BOY TO BE DOING BALLET!
PROMO
BUT, DAD! IT'S A WONDERFUL SPORT! I LOVE IT!
A SPORT! A SPORT?! ALL MY CO-WORKERS MAKE FUN OF ME AT THE OFFICE!
YOU GOT TO ADMIT, THEIR SONS PLAY SOCCER, RUGBY...
...AT WORST, BASKETBALL!
HEY!
HELLO, BRUNO!
HOW'S IT GOING?
ARE YOU DOING ALL RIGHT?
WILL YOU DANCE WITH ME TODAY?
SMAK
SMAK
?
NO! WITH ME!
WITH ME!
SMEK
SMOOCH
SMAK
SHORTLY AFTER...
HEH! HEH! YOUR BOYS MAKE ME LAUGH WITH THEIR CHILDISH BALL GAMES! MY KID'S GOT IT FIGURED OUT--HE'S ALREADY SURROUNDED WITH GIRLS!

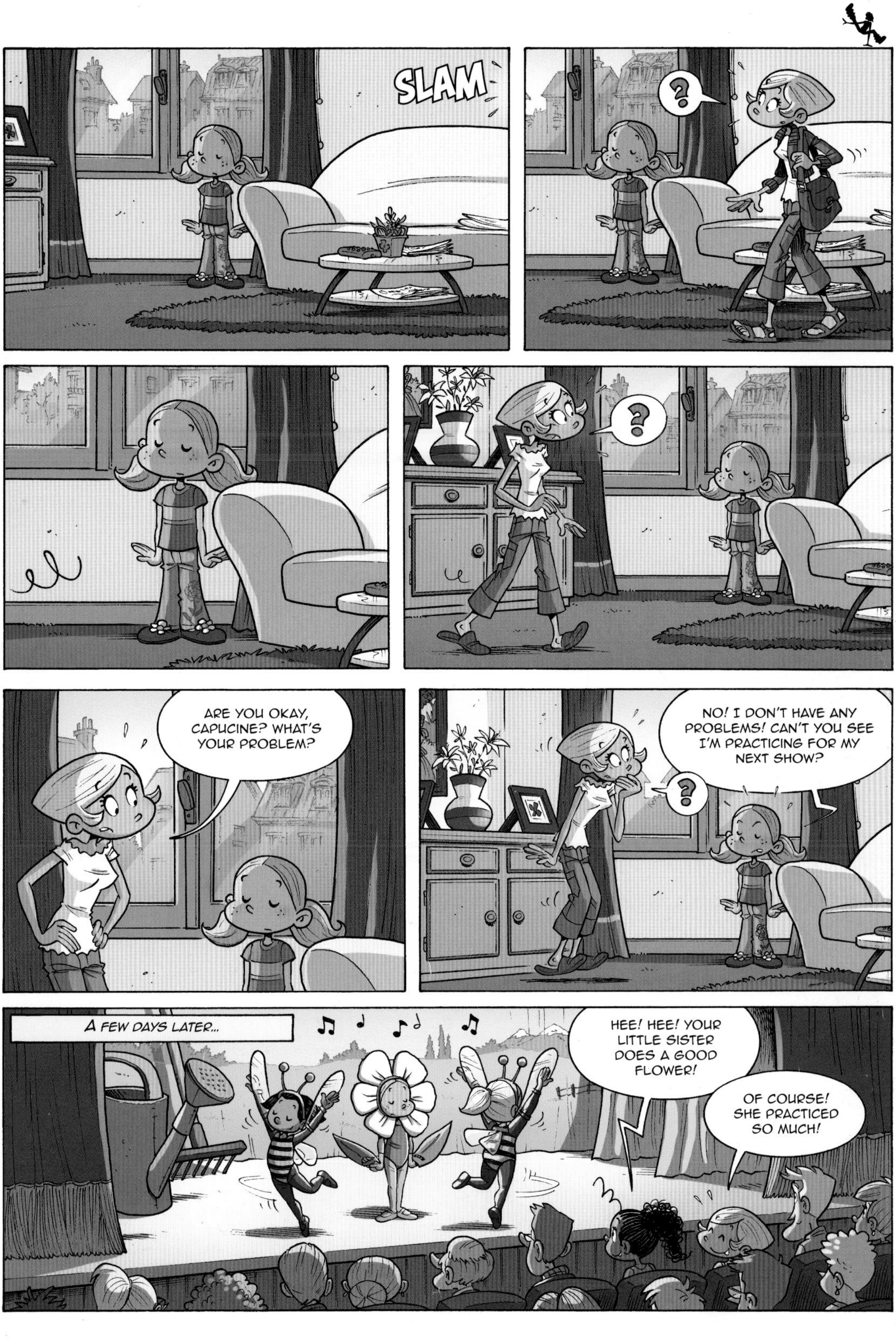
SLAM
?
?
ARE YOU OKAY, CAPUCINE? WHAT'S YOUR PROBLEM?
NO! I DON'T HAVE ANY PROBLEMS! CAN'T YOU SEE I'M PRACTICING FOR MY NEXT SHOW?
?
A FEW DAYS LATER...
HEE! HEE! YOUR LITTLE SISTER DOES A GOOD FLOWER!
OF COURSE! SHE PRACTICED SO MUCH!

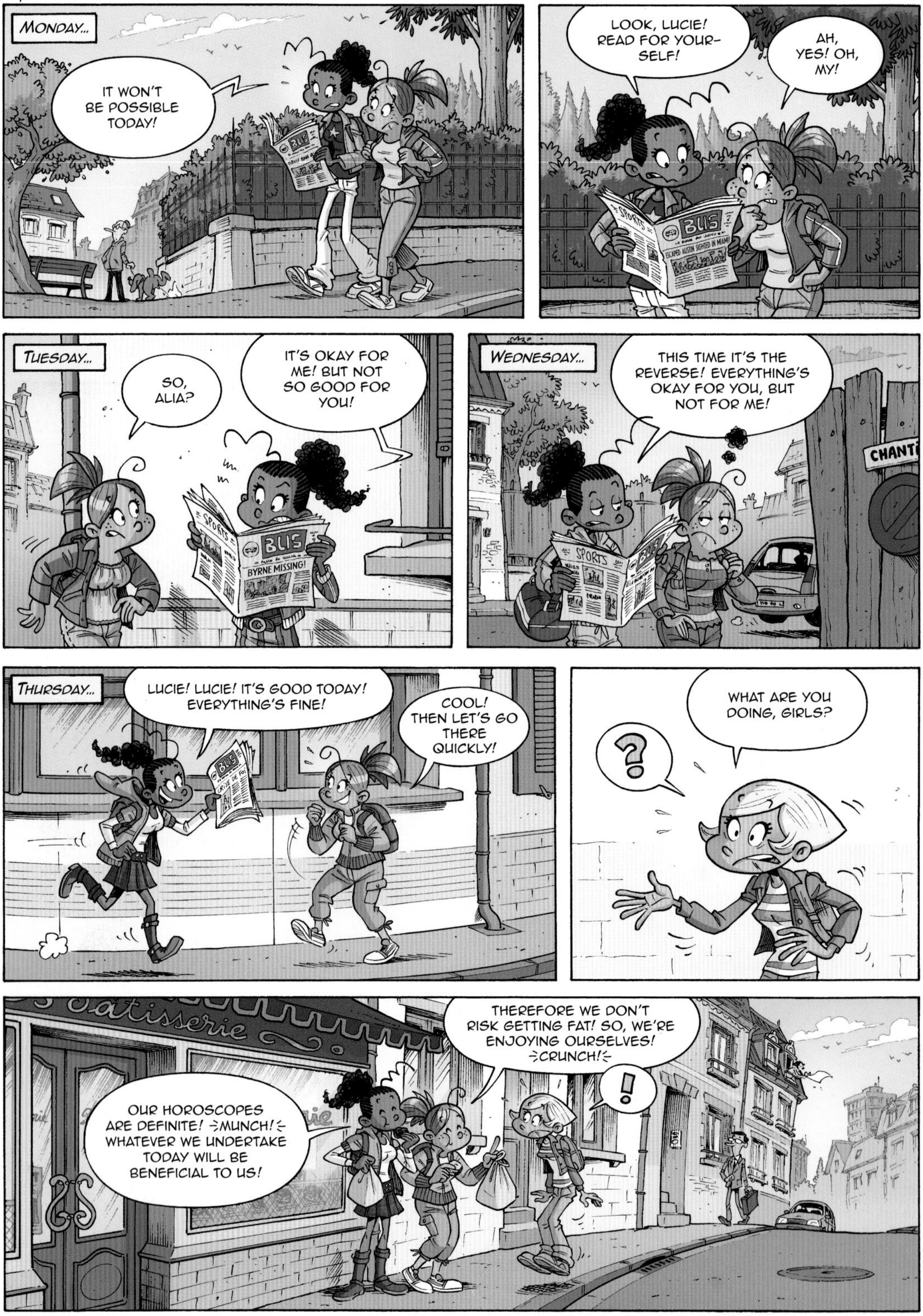
MONDAY...
IT WON'T BE POSSIBLE TODAY!
LOOK, LUCIE! READ FOR YOURSELF!
AH, YES! OH, MY!
BUS
ESCAPED AUSTIN SIGHTED IN MIAMI!
TUESDAY...
SO, ALIA?
IT'S OKAY FOR ME! BUT NOT SO GOOD FOR YOU!
SPORTS
BUS
BYRNE MISSING!
WEDNESDAY...
THIS TIME IT'S THE REVERSE! EVERYTHING'S OKAY FOR YOU, BUT NOT FOR ME!
SPORTS
CHANTI
THURSDAY...
LUCIE! LUCIE! IT'S GOOD TODAY! EVERYTHING'S FINE!
COOL! THEN LET'S GO THERE QUICKLY!
WHAT ARE YOU DOING, GIRLS?
?
Patisserie
THEREFORE WE DON'T RISK GETTING FAT! SO, WE'RE ENJOYING OURSELVES! CRUNCH!
!
OUR HOROSCOPES ARE DEFINITE! MUNCH! WHATEVER WE UNDERTAKE TODAY WILL BE BENEFICIAL TO US!

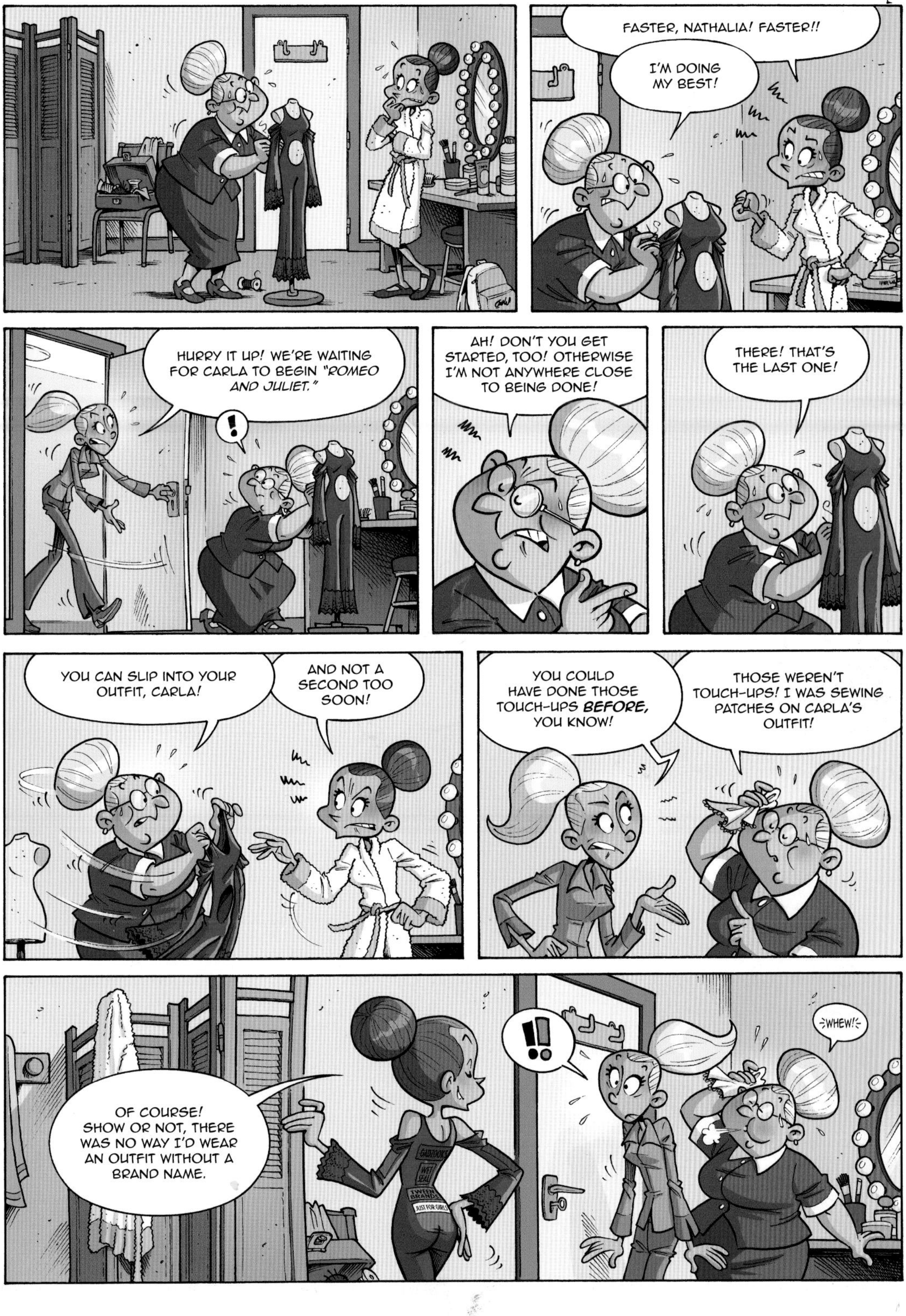
FASTER, NATHALIA! FASTER!!
I'M DOING MY BEST!
HURRY IT UP! WE'RE WAITING FOR CARLA TO BEGIN "ROMEO AND JULIET."
!
AH! DON'T YOU GET STARTED, TOO! OTHERWISE I'M NOT ANYWHERE CLOSE TO BEING DONE!
THERE! THAT'S THE LAST ONE!
YOU CAN SLIP INTO YOUR OUTFIT, CARLA!
AND NOT A SECOND TOO SOON!
YOU COULD HAVE DONE THOSE TOUCH-UPS BEFORE, YOU KNOW!
THOSE WEREN'T TOUCH-UPS! I WAS SEWING PATCHES ON CARLA'S OUTFIT!
OF COURSE! SHOW OR NOT, THERE WAS NO WAY I'D WEAR AN OUTFIT WITHOUT A BRAND NAME.
GADZOOKS
WET SEAL
TWEEN BRANDS
JUST FOR GIRLS
!!
WHEW!

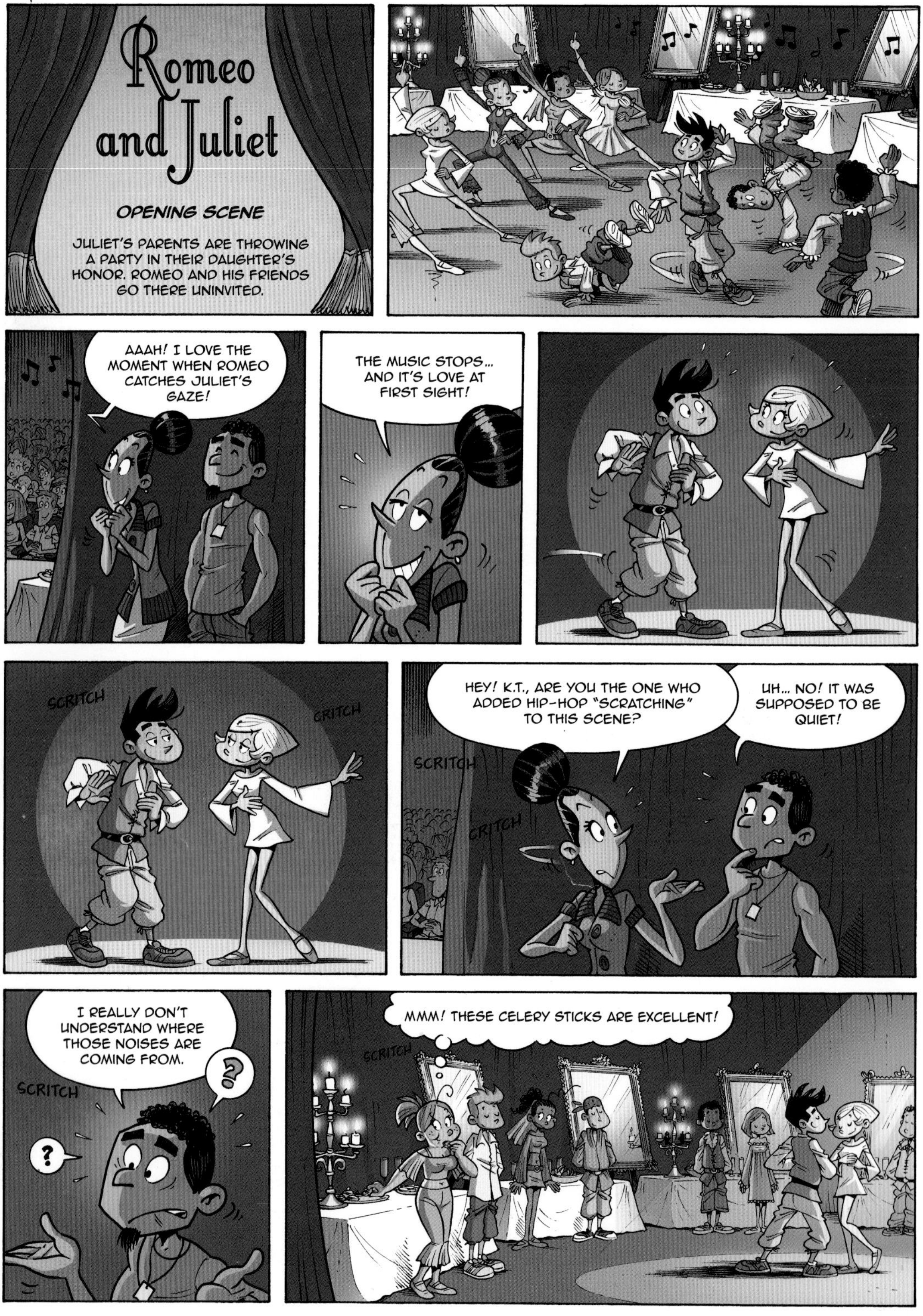
Romeo and Juliet
OPENING SCENE
JULIET'S PARENTS ARE THROWING A PARTY IN THEIR DAUGHTER'S HONOR. ROMEO AND HIS FRIENDS GO THERE UNINVITED.
AAAH! I LOVE THE MOMENT WHEN ROMEO CATCHES JULIET'S GAZE!
THE MUSIC STOPS... AND IT'S LOVE AT FIRST SIGHT!
SCRITCH
CRITCH
HEY! K.T., ARE YOU THE ONE WHO ADDED HIP-HOP "SCRATCHING" TO THIS SCENE?
UH... NO! IT WAS SUPPOSED TO BE QUIET!
SCRITCH
CRITCH
I REALLY DON'T UNDERSTAND WHERE THOSE NOISES ARE COMING FROM.
SCRITCH
?
?
MMM! THESE CELERY STICKS ARE EXCELLENT!
SCRITCH

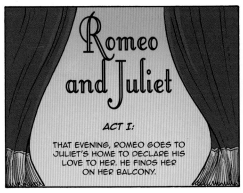

# Romeo and Juliet

### ACT I:

THAT EVENING, ROMEO GOES TO JULIET'S HOME TO DECLARE HIS LOVE TO HER. HE FINDS HER ON HER BALCONY.

BACKSTAGE...

TIM! JULIE! THERE'S BEEN A SLIGHT, LAST-MINUTE CHANGE!

TIM, YOU MUST ENTER ON THIS SIDE! AND YOU, JULIE, MUST GO THROUGH THERE!

ARE YOU SURE, CARLA? I THOUGHT IT WAS THE OPPOSITE!

IT'S BEEN CHANGED, I TELL YOU! HURRY, YOU'RE GOING TO BE LATE!

EH! HEH! I GOT THEM GOOD! THAT'LL TEACH JULIE TO ALWAYS ROB ME OF THE MAIN ROLE!

RUB RUB

EXCELLENT IDEA TO REVERSE ROLES!

ROMEO ON THE BALCONY AND JULIET BELOW! THAT'S WAY MODERN!

CLAP CLAP
BRAVO!
CLAP CLAP
CLAP CLAP
BRAVO!

WAS THAT YOUR IDEA, CARLA? BRAVO! IT'S A HUGE SUCCESS!

YOU'D MAKE A GREAT STAGE DIRECTOR!

CLAP CLAP
CLAP CLAP
CLAP CLAP

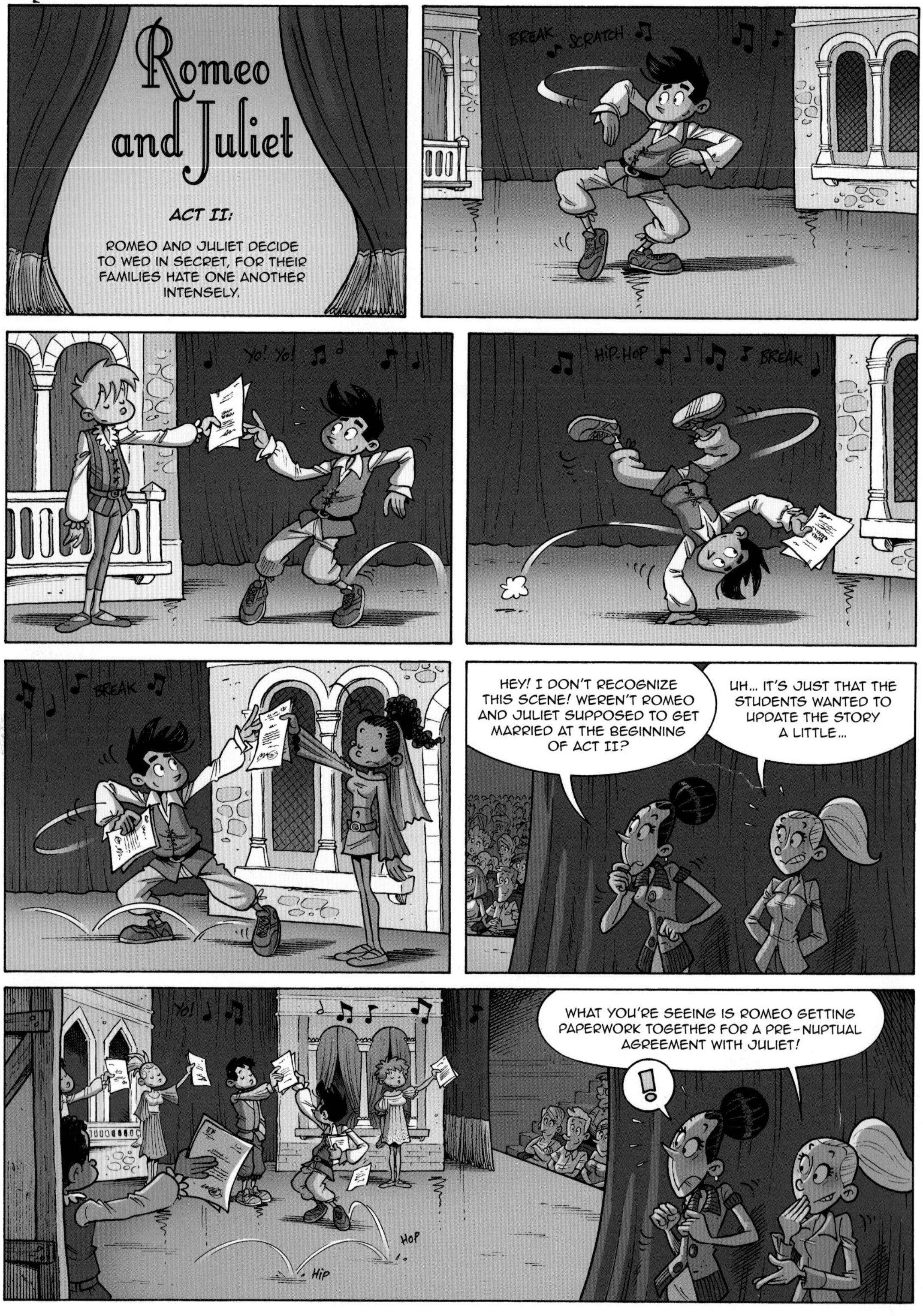
Romeo and Juliet
ACT II:
ROMEO AND JULIET DECIDE TO WED IN SECRET, FOR THEIR FAMILIES HATE ONE ANOTHER INTENSELY.
BREAK
SCRATCH
YO! YO!
HIP-HOP
BREAK
BREAK
HEY! I DON'T RECOGNIZE THIS SCENE! WEREN'T ROMEO AND JULIET SUPPOSED TO GET MARRIED AT THE BEGINNING OF ACT II?
UH... IT'S JUST THAT THE STUDENTS WANTED TO UPDATE THE STORY A LITTLE...
YO!
WHAT YOU'RE SEEING IS ROMEO GETTING PAPERWORK TOGETHER FOR A PRE-NUPTUAL AGREEMENT WITH JULIET!
!
HOP
HIP

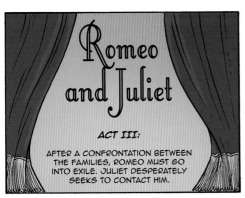

# Romeo and Juliet

## ACT III:

AFTER A CONFRONTATION BETWEEN THE FAMILIES, ROMEO MUST GO INTO EXILE. JULIET DESPERATELY SEEKS TO CONTACT HIM.

HEY! JULIET'S GOT A FUNNY WAY OF TRYING TO SEND A MESSAGE TO ROMEO!

WHY, YES! IT'S STILL THE MODERN VERSION!

SHE'S TRYING TO CALL HIM ON HER CELL PHONE, BUT SHE HAS NO RECEPTION!

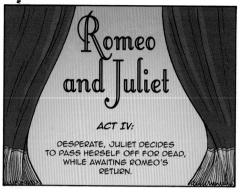

# Romeo and Juliet

**ACT IV:**

DESPERATE, JULIET DECIDES TO PASS HERSELF OFF FOR DEAD, WHILE AWAITING ROMEO'S RETURN.

IF I UNDERSTAND CORRECTLY, JULIET'S TRYING ONE LAST TIME TO REACH ROMEO TO EXPLAIN HER PLAN TO HIM!

THAT'S EXACTLY RIGHT, ANNE!

♪ TADA TADA ♫

AH! THAT'S WHY SHE DOESN'T REACH ROMEO! SHE HAS THE WRONG NUMBER!

UH... NO!

THAT RING WASN'T PLANNED! IT'S SOMEONE WHO MUST HAVE FORGOTTEN TO TURN OFF HIS PHONE!

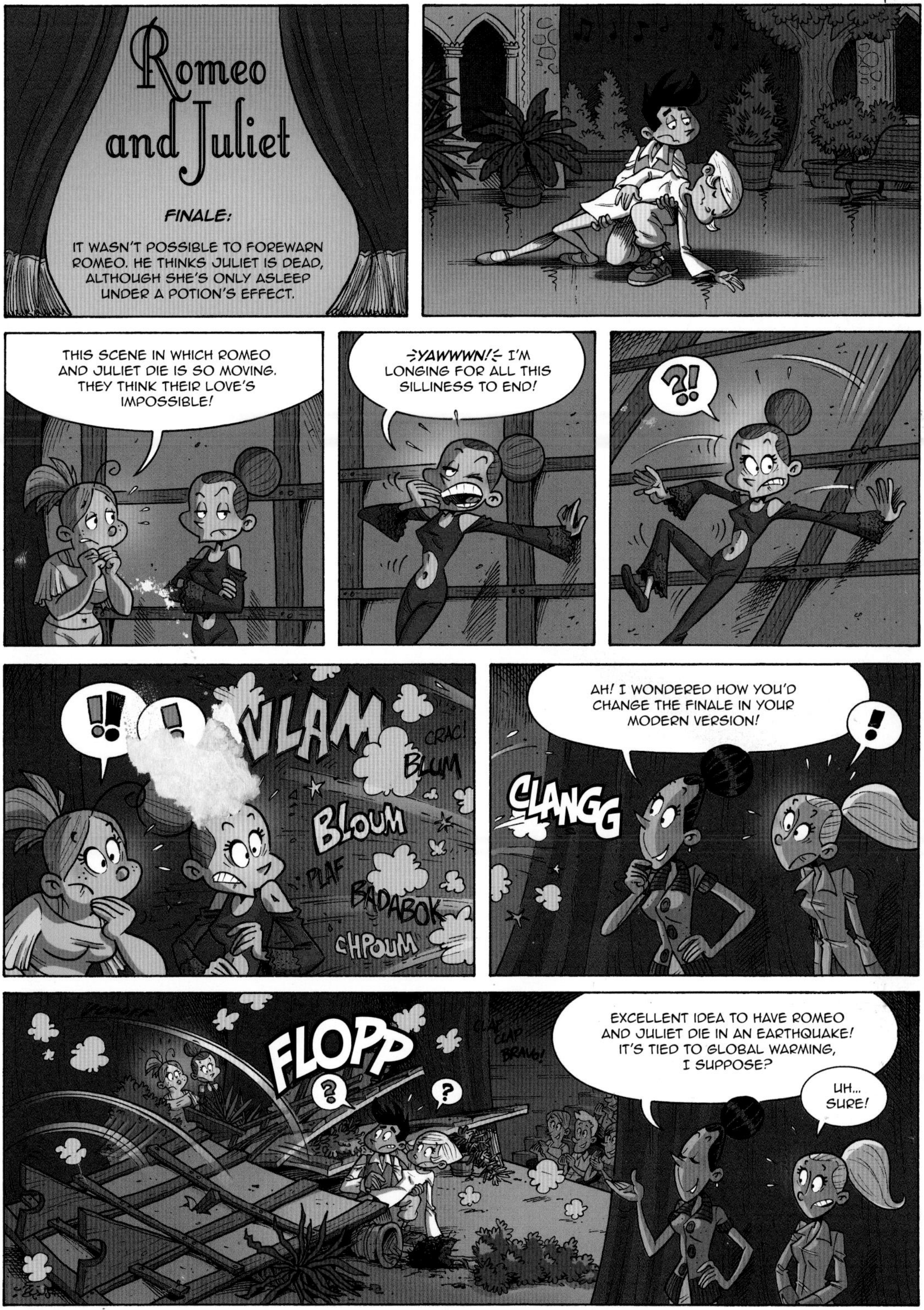

Romeo and Juliet
FINALE:
IT WASN'T POSSIBLE TO FOREWARN ROMEO. HE THINKS JULIET IS DEAD, ALTHOUGH SHE'S ONLY ASLEEP UNDER A POTION'S EFFECT.
THIS SCENE IN WHICH ROMEO AND JULIET DIE IS SO MOVING. THEY THINK THEIR LOVE'S IMPOSSIBLE!
YAWWWN! I'M LONGING FOR ALL THIS SILLINESS TO END!
?!
!!
!
VLAM
CRAC!
BLUM
BLOUM
PLAF
BADABOK
CHPOUM
AH! I WONDERED HOW YOU'D CHANGE THE FINALE IN YOUR MODERN VERSION!
!
CLANGG
FLOPP
?
?
CLAP
CLAP
BRAVO!
EXCELLENT IDEA TO HAVE ROMEO AND JULIET DIE IN AN EARTHQUAKE! IT'S TIED TO GLOBAL WARMING, I SUPPOSE?
UH... SURE!

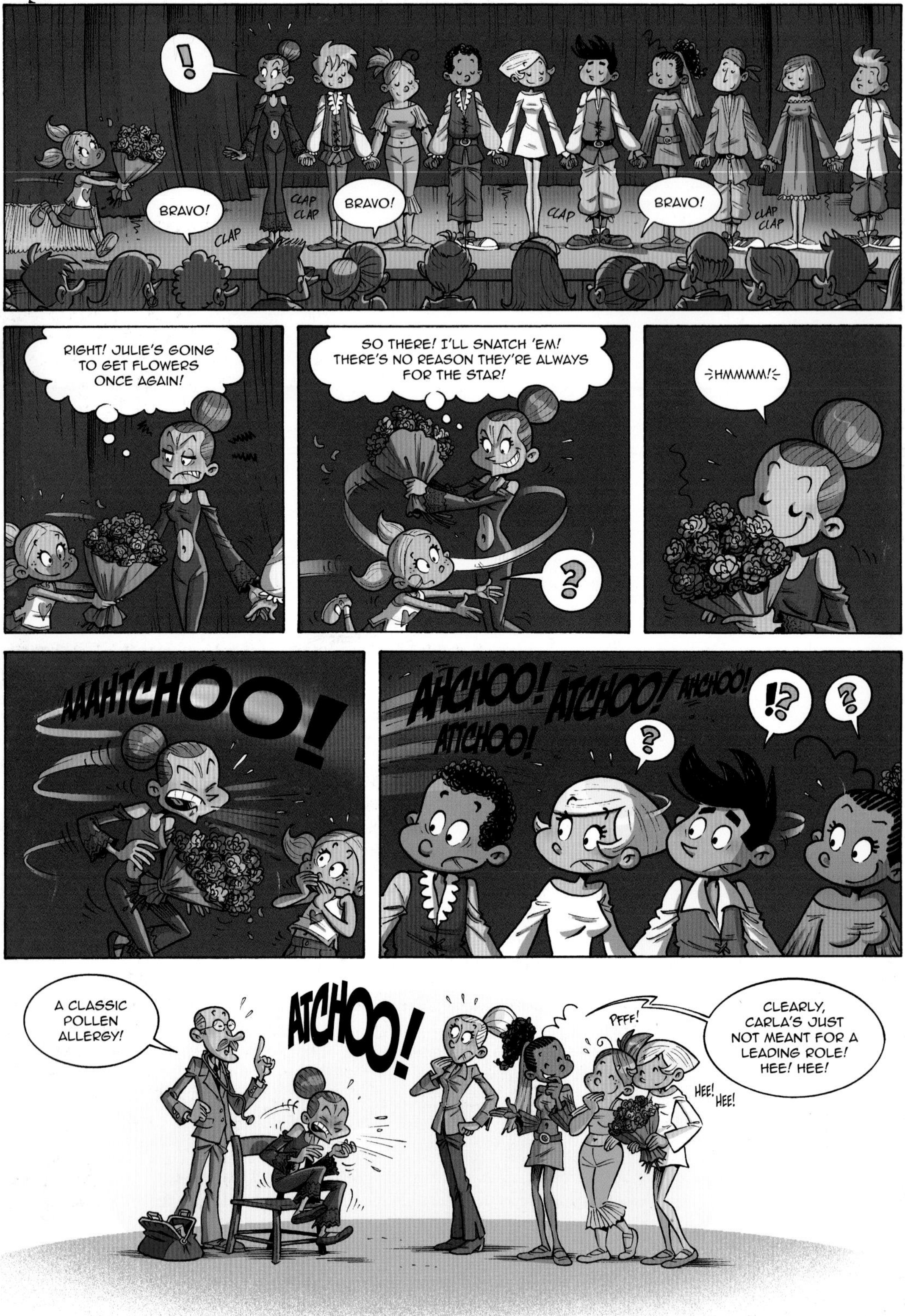
!
BRAVO!
CLAP
CLAP
CLAP
BRAVO!
CLAP
BRAVO!
CLAP
CLAP
RIGHT! JULIE'S GOING TO GET FLOWERS ONCE AGAIN!
SO THERE! I'LL SNATCH 'EM! THERE'S NO REASON THEY'RE ALWAYS FOR THE STAR!
?
HMMMM!
AAAHTCHOOO!
AHCHOO! ATCHOO! AHCHOO!
ATTCHOO!
?
!?
?
A CLASSIC POLLEN ALLERGY!
ATCHOO!
PFFF!
CLEARLY, CARLA'S JUST NOT MEANT FOR A LEADING ROLE! HEE! HEE!
HEE! HEE!

# WATCH OUT FOR PAPERCUTZ ™

Welcome to the somewhat smaller second DANCE CLASS graphic novel by Crip & Béka. I'm Jim Salicrup, a lapsed dance student and Editor-in-Chief of Papercutz, the toe-tapping troupe that is dedicated to publishing great graphic novels for all ages. I'm here to answer the eternal question, does size matter?

For those of you who picked up our premiere DANCE CLASS graphic novel, you may have noticed that instead of being a whopping eight inches by ten inches, this volume of DANCE CLASS is a mere six and a half inches by nine inches. The key thing is that we're still the exact same amount of pages! So, why, you may be wondering, did we change? It seems, according to the publishing experts at our distributor, the mighty Macmillan, consumers of a certain age are very reluctant to purchase anything they think may be intended for younger customers. In other words, a twelve-year-old is not interested in buying something that seems designed for a six-year-old. And it turns out, that in the wild and wacky world of children's book publishing, the bigger the size of the book, in terms of height and width, the younger the intended audience. You can see what a serious problem that could pose for Papercutz—a publisher, as we said, devoted to reaching all ages.

Well, the more we explored this particular problem, the more we discovered! It turns out that the opposite of that rule doesn't apply. While older kids will avoid material for younger kids, younger kids can't wait to get their hands on stuff intended for older kids. So whatever fears we had of possibly alienating our younger fans proved to be unfounded. Thus was born our new smaller-than-ever format for DANCE CLASS. We sincerely hope you enjoy it—no matter how old you are!

In another size-related matter, there seemed to be a few folks who were concerned that we might inadvertently be creating problems regarding body-issues for some members of our audience. Specifically, there's been criticism that the character Lucie in DANCE CLASS is not drawn to look more overweight, and that if she is portrayed as the "fat" girl, girls who weigh even more than her, will have an issue about how they look.

Well, first let me say that, while we're not psychologists at Papercutz, we are sensitive to anything that may offend or cause problems for our audience. As for Lucie, I first have to say, I love Lucie! Other than Carla meanly calling Lucie "chubby" in DANCE CLASS #1, there's no reason to think of Lucie as being "fat." Like many people, myself included, she'd like to lose a few pounds, but she has a "sweet tooth." Clearly, compared to all the other characters in DANCE CLASS, Lucie is heavier, but she is by no stretch of the imagination overweight, nor is she portrayed that way in the comics. In fact, in a humorous sequence in this very book, Lucie, and Alia, are seen coming up with a silly scheme to avoid "getting fat." Something they wouldn't be doing if they thought they already had a weight problem.

Furthermore, taking a dance class is a form of exercise—a very vigorous form of exercise. Therefore, it makes sense that the DANCE CLASS students are all in very good physical shape. Now does that mean we're portraying this particular body type as the ideal, and implying if you don't look like this, there's something wrong with you? I don't believe so, but I welcome feedback on this subject. You can email me directly at salicrup@papercutz.com or send snail-mail to me at Jim Salicrup, Papercutz, 160 Broadway, Suite 700, East Wing, New York, NY 10038.

As corny as it may sound, we at Papercutz love comics, we love dance, and we love you. The last thing we'd ever want to do is hurt someone's feelings. After all, we want you to come back for the next DANCE CLASS graphic novel-- #3 "African Folk Fever"! Until then, keep on dancin'!

Thanks, Jim

# Check Out These Other Graphic Novels from PAPERCUTZ™

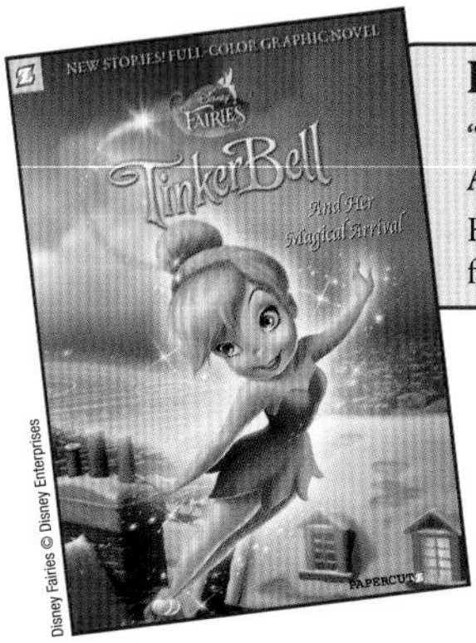

NEW STORIES! FULL-COLOR GRAPHIC NOVEL
Disney FAIRIES
TinkerBell
And Her Magical Arrival
PAPERCUTZ



**DISNEY FAIRIES #9**
**"Tinker Bell and her Magical Arrival"**
Four magical tales featuring the fairies from Pixie Hollow!

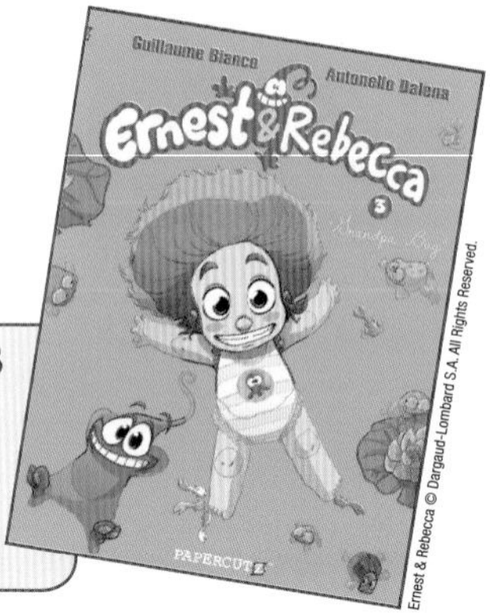

Guillaume Bianco
Antonello Dalena
Ernest & Rebecca
3
PAPERCUTZ



**ERNEST & REBECCA #3**
**"Grandpa Bug"**
A 6 ½ year old girl and her microbial buddy against the world!

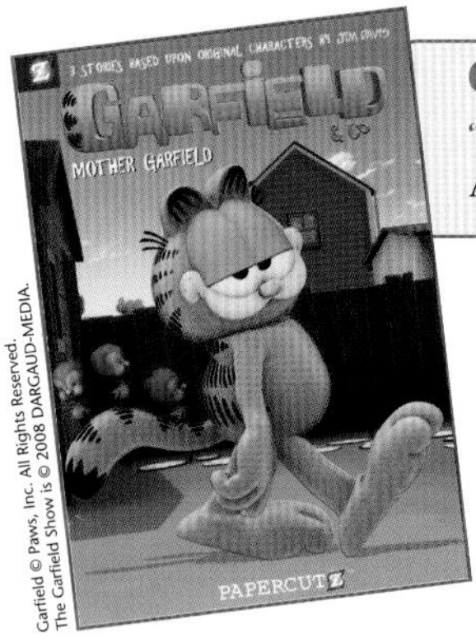

GARFIELD & Co
MOTHER GARFIELD
PAPERCUTZ



**GARFIELD & Co #6**
**"Mother Garfield"**
As seen on the Cartoon Network!

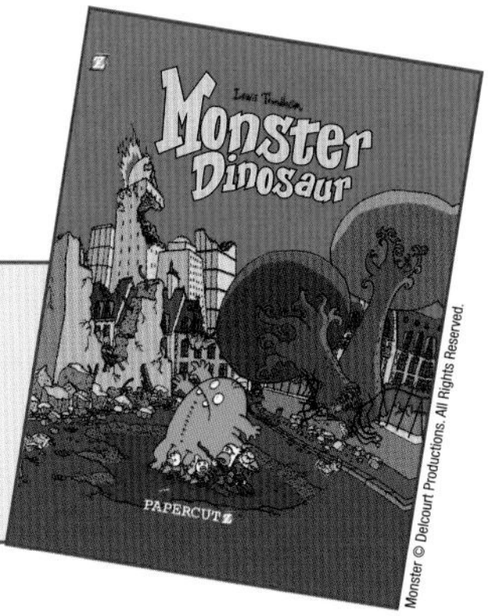

Monster Dinosaur
PAPERCUTZ



**MONSTER #3**
**"Monster Dinosaur"**
The almost normal adventures of an almost ordinary family... with a pet monster!

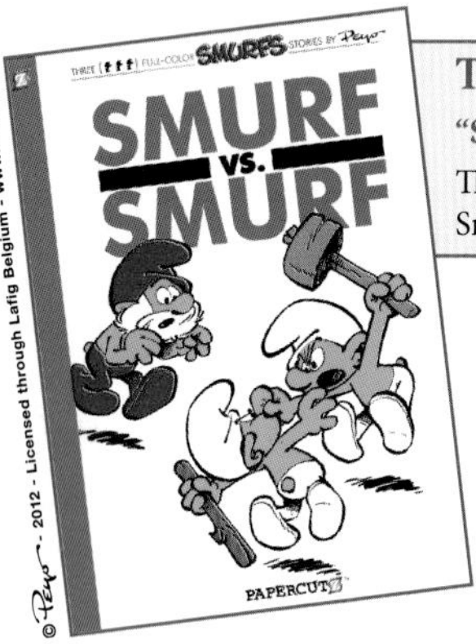

SMURFS
SMURF VS. SMURF
PAPERCUTZ



**THE SMURFS #12**
**"Smurf Vs. Smurf"**
There's big trouble brewing in the Smurfs Village!

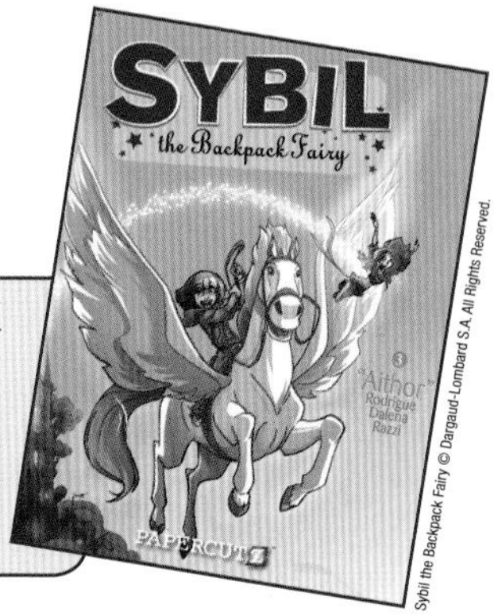

SYBIL
the Backpack Fairy
3
"Aithor"
Rodrigue
Dalena
Razzi
PAPERCUTZ



**SYBIL THE BACKPACK FAIRY #3**
**"Aithor"**
What's cooler than a fairy in your backpack? How about a flying horse?!

Available at better booksellers everywhere!

Or order directly from us! DISNEY FAIRIES is available in paperback for $7.99, in hardcover for $11.99; ERNEST & REBECCA is $11.99 in hardcover only; GARFIELD & Co is available in hardcover only for $7.99; MONSTER is available in hardcover only for $9.99; THE SMURFS are available in paperback for $5.99, in hardcover for $10.99; and SYBIL THE BACKPACK FAIRY is available in hardcover only for $11.99.

Please add $4.00 for postage and handling for the first book, add $1.00 for each additional book.

Please make check payable to NBM Publishing. Send to: PAPERCUTZ, 160 Broadway, Suite 700, East Wing, New York, NY 10038
(1-800-886-1223)

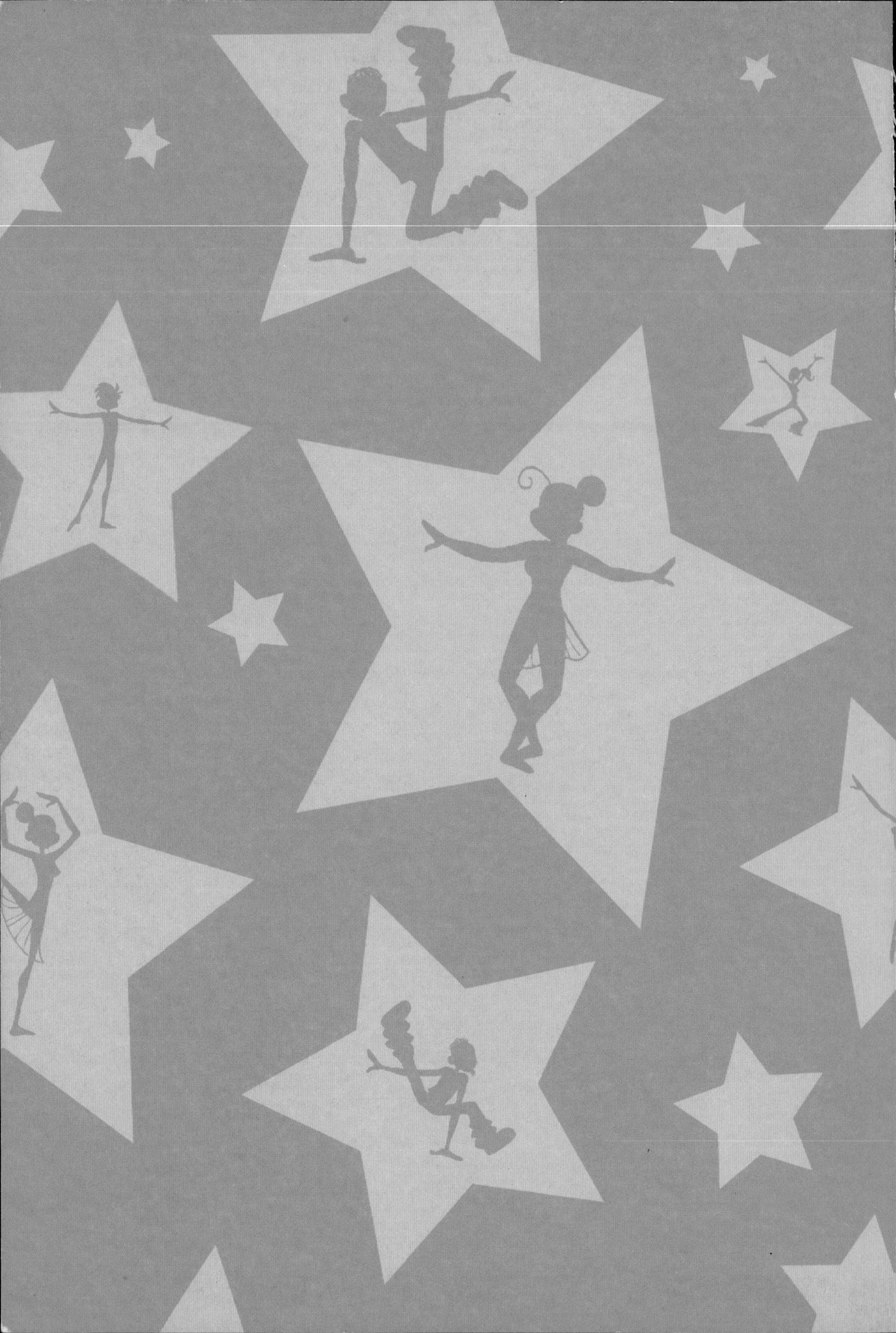